THE DARK HILL

Also by Rae Foley

THE
DARK
HILL

A RED BADGE NOVEL OF SUSPENSE

by Rae Foley

DODD, MEAD
& COMPANY
New York

Library of Congress Cataloging in Publication Data

The dark hill.

(A Red badge novel of suspense)
I.   Title.
PZ3.D426Dap [PS3554.E56]   813'.5'4   74-34117
ISBN 0-396-07081-7

For Jean and Cecil Covalt
with affection and gratitude
for much kindness and sunshine
in Port Hueneme

"We've each a darkling hill to climb. . . ."
—EDWIN ARLINGTON ROBINSON

THE DARK HILL

One

It was Allan who referred to himself as A Friend of the Family. The caps were his. He did it one Saturday afternoon when I went into his room to bring him some hot gingerbread I had just baked. It was the first time I had been there since he moved in, and I noticed that he had added nothing of his own except for some toilet articles, neatly arranged on the old-fashioned dresser, a record player with an impressive stack of records, and a framed photograph of three boys of about my own age, eighteen, posed against a background of palm trees.

After a moment's study I recognized the one in the middle as Allan, taken a good ten years earlier. On one side of him was a narrow-shouldered youth wearing a brilliant Hawaiian shirt, which did not accord with his sober face. The third boy had flung back his head and he was apparently shouting with laughter.

"Just some guys I knew at Princeton," Allan said, in answer to my question. "I don't know why I keep the thing around."

1

"Who is the laughing one?"

"Girls would always ask about him first. That is Tommy Eakins, The Playboy of the Western World."

Something in his tone made me say quickly, "And the other one?"

"Don't you recognize him? You should. He's photographed often enough. No, I suppose he's changed a bit in ten years; outwardly, at least. That is Fillmore Hatfield the Third."

"The millionaire?" I asked, awed.

"Multimillionaire. The Man Who Has Everything. He's the one, of course, who paid for that Hawaiian vacation."

"He must be very generous," I said, reacting to the cold dislike in Allan's voice.

"Generosity or charity or investment. It's never easy to tell with our Fillmore."

Because I had never known Allan to display any animosity, I was uneasy, as the young are when their simplistic images of people are clouded. "And you?"

"Oh," and he grinned at me, "in an old-fashioned play I'd be listed as A Friend of the Family."

"I think family friends are the nicest."

Allan entered our lives when my father's business was in the doldrums and my mother, promptly going into action, advertised for rent a furnished room with its own bath and separate entrance, suitable for a quiet gentleman. The following day Allan appeared on the doorstep of our little house in Red Bank, New Jersey.

A quiet gentleman. Those words summed up Allan Drummond. He was tall, thin rather than slender, neatly dressed, closely shaven, his hair cut short, his linen immaculate. He did not have a memorable face, but no one could mistake his kindness. He introduced himself to my mother, betraying his surprise when she insisted that she was the lady of the house, because she looked so preposterously young. People constantly mistook us for sisters, which embarrassed her as though she had been caught doing something unseemly.

Allan explained that he had a new business, as unsteady on its feet as a newborn kitten. He designed and made ceramics in a small shop in Red Bank, where he had also been sleeping, or at least bunking down in a back room. He did his own selling. It was not, he admitted with his pleasant smile, profitable at the moment, but he had great hopes for it and, anyhow, he enjoyed doing it. He'd be glad to provide a letter from his bank and social references. The latter was a euphemism for a guarantee of his respectability, though his appearance and manner carried their own built-in guarantee.

When I said so, my father flipped a finger lightly against my cheek. "You always simplify, Kate. Like your mother. 'A quiet gentleman.' That sums up the new lodger for you both, but no human being could ever be as easily labeled as that. Even a coin has two sides, and a man has a lot more angles."

My father operated a small real estate agency, a business for which he could hardly have been worse fitted, as he was totally lacking in aggression and more likely to point out the defects than the advantages of the property he was supposed to be renting or selling. My mother was too wise to criticize or make suggestions, which is why ours was a happy household, but she handled the billing and the paper work without fuss or bustle and with an efficiency that always surprised people because she had such a misleadingly helpless appearance.

As a result of the closely knit partnership between our parents, my brother Mike and I were left alone a great deal. As Mike was ten years younger than I, it was necessary to be assured of the reliability of the new tenant whose rent meant, if not steak for dinner, at least the difference between hamburg and spaghetti.

Actually, Allan was the kind of tenant anyone might dream of. He was quiet and unobtrusive, he kept his room as neat as a pin, and, unlike my parents, he usually spent the evenings at home. We could hear the muted sound of his record player, which was my first indication of the complexity of his personality, as his collection ranged from Bach to Rock.

On my mother's birthday he diffidently presented her with a ceramic portrait, which delighted her. It was a tiny but wildly alive woman, about four inches high, whose red hair was blowing as though she was running, apron strings flying as though she was about to take off into orbit, and the wide, eager eyes that were so characteristic of her. My mother promptly removed from the mantel a Steuben bowl, which had been a wedding present, and gave the ceramic figure the place of honor.

"He's caught the very essence of you, Kathy," my father said. "The man has real talent. I'd never have suspected the existence of so much imagination and insight. He could make himself famous if he just knew how to market his wares."

"Like you," my mother said lovingly.

It's odd how little Allan told us about himself during the three years he lived in our house, though, almost imperceptibly, he became one of the family. He was the kindest man I had ever known. From the beginning my little brother

4

became his shadow, admired him, emulated him, and tagged along whenever he was allowed to do so.

As Mike grew older, Allan taught him to play chess and to listen to classical music with enthusiasm and understanding. He even convinced him that there was something more exciting to do than watch ham actors shoot blank cartridges at each other on a television screen and inoculated him with a love of reading, not science fiction and factual books, but the great fiction that furnishes the mind and stimulates the imagination.

He even offered to take him to the workshop where he designed, modeled, and fired his ceramics and, hopefully, sold them. This he did over my mother's protests.

"Mike is a bull in the china closet."

"Mike is the most trustworthy human being I've ever known. If I tell him to be careful, he'll be careful. Especially," and Allan grinned, "when he knows I'll break his neck if he isn't."

Mike grinned in return and trotted happily off with Allan. And that was the first time Mike disappeared. Allan was almost frantic when he came home that evening without him. He had been occupied with a potential buyer and when he looked around, Mike was gone. He was nowhere in the shop. No one on the street had seen a small boy with flaming red hair. He had left no message.

The color faded from my mother's pretty face, which was usually as flushed and sweet as a wild rose. She clutched at my father's arm.

"Don't go into a tailspin," he said calmly. "Mike always has his wits about him. If he'd had an accident," and my mother's hand tightened, "we'd have heard about it. If he

5

doesn't show up by midnight, I'll call the Missing Persons Bureau."

"Midnight!" my mother wailed.

"No one kidnaped the boy. Anyone would know we couldn't scrape up ransom money."

"Then what could have happened to him?"

"Well," my father drawled, "knowing Mike, I'd guess that something aroused his curiosity"—there was a collective groan—"and when he has thoroughly satisfied it, he'll come home."

We didn't have to wait until midnight. At eight o'clock Mike showed up, almost prancing with self-satisfaction, and shouted for Allan and some food. When he had partially appeased his appetite, he turned to the anxious Allan. "You know what?"

"Where have you been?" That was a chorus.

Mike was so pleased with himself that he almost burst. He looked at Allan. "You remember the guy in the brown suit who sort of cornered you to talk?"

Allan nodded. "A customer."

"Did he buy anything?" Mike demanded.

"He was just looking around. He said he'd be back."

"Betcha he won't." Mike was triumphant. "He came in with another guy who stood back until your attention was nailed and then he began to prowl around. He acted—queer, so I kept an eye on him. And then he shot out his hand and slipped three of those pieces of yours into his pockets: the old man leaning over a book and you can tell he doesn't know what's going on around him because he's so interested; the girl in the bikini, who is sort of showing off; and the fat man laughing so you can't help laughing with him."

6

"Well?"

"Well, he strolled out of the shop and I went after him because it was sort of odd. You were selling those pieces for eighty-nine cents wholesale and a guy didn't need to steal them. Anyhow, I had my allowance for last week and this week too, so I followed him to New York and a joint on Broadway where he sold them to the manager of a novelty shop for eight dollars apiece. So I hung around and trailed him home and he got mail out of a box in a Sixty-sixth Street apartment with the name of Harry Travis on it, and the shop he sold to is the Avant-Garde Curiosity Shop."

No one ever had a better audience, and Mike's story was followed by a round of applause, which he accepted as his due. There was never any false modesty about Mike.

"I think," Allan said, "I'd better take you into partner-ship."

"I think," Mother said, bursting with pride but trying to look severe, "you had better go to bed."

"I think," Mike said, sticking to fundamentals, "I'd better have another piece of chocolate cake. Gosh, I've been a busy man."

When he had finally gone to bed, weary but triumphant, Mother said, "Allan, it makes me furious to have you get gypped that way. You need someone to parlay your talents properly."

"Someone like you," Allan said, smiling at her.

"Or Kate," Dad said. "You're just like your mother. At eighty you'll still both look twenty years younger than you are. You're both so pretty and fragile in appearance that no one will believe you are practical." He added with pretended disapproval, "Dishearteningly so." Then, in the unlikely event that my mother had taken him seriously, he gave her a hug. "You know what? You're fun to be married to." He smiled. "Kate will be too."

Over their heads Allan looked at me, half-smiling, half-rueful. In all the time he had lived at our house, he had never asked me for a date. To me he seemed middle-aged and he knew it.

"In a more stately age," he commented, "Kate would have called me 'sir.' "

My father looked at him sharply but made no comment as Allan said good night and went to his own room. Later I could hear my parents talking, my mother's light voice protesting, "What on earth are you trying to do, Bob? Allan is too old for Kate, and she's too young to marry."

"You were seventeen when I married you. Granted it was a grave mistake . . ."

II

As my mother spent so much time in the office, trying to hold the business together, I naturally took over the housework and cooking and shopping, which, with soaring prices and our limited income, was a challenge and practically a life-work in itself. And I had dates, of course—lots of dates. I was rarely home in the evenings, which is one reason why I saw comparatively little of Allan. All in all, that was a happy time and carefree, though financially we just scraped through, but we were all doing what we really wanted and there is no satisfactory substitute for that.

I was living at high pitch and what seemed to me a perfect whirl of gaiety. I'd had two proposals of marriage but consid-

8

ered neither of them seriously, though I was proud as Punch at being wanted. At twenty-one I was too often taken for fifteen, so I was dazzled at the idea of being considered old and mature enough for marriage.

The first major change in our lives came about as a direct result of Mike's pursuit of Allan's thief. At my mother's insistence, Allan went to the police with Mike's story. He did it with reluctance. There was so little at stake, he said, and he couldn't afford a lawyer, and what could he hope to achieve?

Envious people often say that all success is a matter of luck or breaks, which my father thought was hooey, but in Allan's case luck did intervene. The day he went to the police station, accompanied by a starry-eyed Mike, a young reporter was hanging around, looking for crumbs. Instead, he found a feast. He built up the story of the boy detective and even got some pictures of Allan's ceramics in the paper. Allan was more embarrassed than pleased, but my mother was delighted.

"You wait and see," she prophesied, "something is bound to come of all this publicity. Your big chance is just around the corner."

And she was right. Only a few days later Allan informed us that some New York man had read the story, been impressed by the ceramics, and had come out to New Jersey to look them over. As a result of his report to his principal, the latter offered to provide him with a Madison Avenue display room, a sales assistant, and bigger and better equipment for his workshop in Red Bank, so that he could be prepared to turn out large orders. He also offered to get some useful publicity into trade journals and art magazines. With such

9

a setup, Allan would soon have a thriving business and a growing reputation.

We were all delighted, especially Mike, who felt that he was responsible for the whole thing. And when Allan had moved to an apartment on Manhattan, it was Mike who missed him most, though we all felt a gap in the house without him, and a serious gap in our income, though we rejoiced in his good fortune and would not have had it otherwise.

It was almost six months before we saw or heard from Allan Drummond. When he did come back, the whole fabric of our lives had been torn apart. On their way home from the office one evening my father and mother were struck down by muggers, and their skulls cracked by a vicious beating, though neither of them would or could have put up any resistance. For the double murder the muggers got two dollars and twenty-four cents and the freedom to strike again, as they were never apprehended.

It takes time to absorb a loss like that, to react to the shock, to cope with the grief, to accept the situation, to start living again. Living in a different way. But there was no time. We did not actually live from hand to mouth, but we did live from month to month. Something had to be decided at once.

As soon as he read of the deaths of our parents—a small news item because they were not important people and Red Bank is not an important town and mugging is not an important crime—Allan telephoned, greatly upset, saying that he was on his way. Being Allan, he wasted no time in useless sympathy and empty consolation. He took over, handled the police inquiry, arranged for the funeral, helped to close up the real estate business—there wasn't much to be done—and

10

then settled down, his manner carefully practical, because he was aware of how close I was to losing control.

"What next, Kate?"

When I looked my question, he explained, "You and Mike can't go on living here alone, you know. You can't keep up the expenses of the house and you certainly can't take the risk of an unknown tenant, not a couple of kids like you."

"I don't see why we can't stay here. We've lived here all our lives and we have lots of friends."

"I can give you some reasons: food, taxes, electricity, water, gas, clothing, sewage and trash disposal, clothing, doctor bills, transportation. And that's just a start. Mike's only eleven. Haven't you any family who could take him?"

"No, we haven't, and, anyhow, Mike stays with me. That's final."

"I want to stay with Kate; she's okay." Which, from Mike, was an accolade.

Allan's kind face was distressed. In the past six months he had aged in some intangible way. Evidently Manhattan did not agree with him. "You're much too young to take on responsibility for Mike. And what do you expect to live on?"

"There has to be some way out," I said stubbornly. "I'm of age, in perfect health, and reasonably intelligent. There has to be some sort of job I can fill and earn enough to keep Mike and me."

Mike went out of the room. I knew he found it unbearable to be a burden, and he needed to work it out for himself. I didn't attempt to stop him; I knew him so well.

When he had gone, Allan stretched out his hand and took mine. "Look here, Kate, I didn't mean to say this now. I intended to wait until you were—older, until I could get you

11

to see me as something more than just a family friend. And now when you are left alone, it seems like taking an unfair advantage. Just the same, will you marry me? I'd be good to you, and Mike likes me." There was something unexpectedly humble in his tone as he added diffidently, "I'd take good care of him, you know."

Tears spilled down my cheeks. "How kind you are, Allan!"

He smiled wryly. "Is that the way you see it? Actually, this is selfish of me. I'm taking advantage of your position to offer you a kind of security."

"Security?"

"Not just that, of course." He stood up abruptly, drawing me into his arms. "I love you, Kate. I've loved you all along, but you seemed such a kid. I didn't want—Please marry me, Kate. Now. Right away. As soon as we can get a license. I have a nice little apartment on Riverside Drive. You'd like it. And Mike would be sure of a good education; I'd take care of that."

I'd never been so close to him before, so that all the details of his face and eyes were magnified: hollows under his eyes as though he had not been sleeping well; a broken vein in one cheek; a faint shadow on his upper lip.

"Allan?" I didn't know what question I was asking, what I was demanding of him.

"Don't say no." There was something curiously desperate in his tone. I had never before suspected there was such deep feeling behind that calm façade. "I love you so much." He bent his head, seeking my mouth, but I found myself thrusting him away.

"I'm sorry, Allan. Truly sorry. And proud you want me. So proud. Only—I just can't."

He managed to smile. "Why should I be so lucky? Don't let it worry you, Kate. It was just an idea. Now let's put our so-called minds together and see what we can dream up. Where were we when I got off the beam? Oh, the sordid business of financing a life for you and Mike. You haven't ever held a job. I'll help you sell the house and you might as well get rid of the furniture. It's about had it."

"Don't you know anyone who might give me a job?"

"God knows I'd hire you tomorrow, but right now the business is just beginning to roll and there's no work for another person."

"What about that friend of yours, the rich one in the picture taken in Hawaii? Couldn't he find a place for me somewhere, with all those businesses he owns?"

"Fillmore could support all of Red Bank and never notice it," Allan said, and I had never heard him use that tone, "but I'm damned if I'm taking any more favors from him. Fillmore and his little charities!"

Something in his manner prevented me from asking questions. "Well, what about the other one in the picture?"

"Tommy Eakins?" The scowl faded and Allan laughed. "Well, hardly. So far as I know, he doesn't work, he doesn't approve of it. Never knew such a guy for getting out from under." He rubbed his forehead thoughtfully, "But his father —" He rubbed harder, as though stimulating thought. "Eakins is as nice a fellow as you'd want to know. Sort of impractical, like your father," and Allan smiled to assure me that no criticism was intended. "He has a small outfit, which he tries to handle himself, as Tommy is never around when needed. It's possible—of course, I don't suppose he could pay much."

"Well," I admitted candidly, "I'm not worth much. Whatever it is would be better than nothing, and in the evenings I could be brushing up on my typing and looking around to see what the possibilities are. And we wouldn't need a lot; I'm used to managing on very little."

Allan got up, looking down at me, frowning. Then his face cleared. "Of course, Tommy is never there, so you ought to be all right. Well, what are we waiting for?" He reached for the telephone.

Two

On Monday morning I went to the Eakins Travel Agency in the heart of the Village. At my insistence I was unaccompanied, though Allan had wanted to go with me. Greenwich Village was hardly safe for a young girl alone, he said, worried. I laughed at him. If I was going to work and live there, I might as well get used to it, first as last. Anyhow, I had the conviction common to most youngsters that nothing could happen to me.

That morning for the first time Mike had clung to me. He knew how much hinged on my trip to New York and that our familiar life was threatened.

"Everything is going to be all right," I assured him. "This is Allan's idea, you know."

"You think a lot of Allan, don't you?"

"Well, of course. I couldn't get along without Allan."

When I had sent Mike off to school, I bundled into my warmest clothes, pulled a wool cap down over my ears because the day was cold and raw as March days can be, with a cruelly biting wind. I noticed that there was a slit in one of my gloves and reminded myself to keep it out of sight.

I took a Fifth Avenue bus and was so excited that I almost forgot my nervousness at facing my first prospective employer, on whom so much depended. In spite of the dirty snow the city looked beautiful to me with its soaring buildings, the wide avenue with slow-moving traffic, and the big hotels near the Washington Square Arch.

I walked along Eighth Street, the main stem of the Village, staring round-eyed at the artists' supply shops, the bookshops with their self-consciously esoteric titles, the little restaurants geared for tourists rather than the people who lived there, the long-haired girls and bearded boys scurrying along with heads bent against the force of the wind.

I had to inquire several times before I found the little street where the Eakins Travel Agency sign was propped in a first-floor window of a two-story and basement building which had once been a private home. On one side there was an alley running through the block, and next door was a run-down apartment building. One thing was obvious, even to my inexperienced eyes: the Eakins Travel Agency was not a flourishing concern.

I went up four steps, pushed open the outside door which admitted me grudgingly, the hinges squeaking as though they had never known oil, and found myself in a dingy hallway with uncarpeted stairs on the left and on the right a couple of mailboxes, with the word EAKINS on a big card above them. One box was marked "Agency" and the other "Personal," so I gathered that Mr. Eakins lived above his business, such as it was.

There was only one door with a sign reading EAKINS TRAVEL AGENCY. Below it was a smaller sign, "Knock and

16

walk in." I followed instructions, trying to look a lot more confident than I felt. My heart was thumping and I was breathless. I knew my nose was as red as my hair, and my eyes were watery from the March gale.

I had been warned that this was no prosperous business, but I had not expected to find it on its last legs. There was a lot to be done here. But by the time I walked into the Eakins Travel Agency, it was already too late to prevent any of the events that followed. The fuse had been lighted and the situation was already on the verge of explosion.

There was no one in the outer office, which held two desks, one with a covered typewriter and a telephone; the other strewn with travel folders, a chair hopefully beside it for any customers. The walls were hung with pictures whose edges were curling.

From behind the half-opened inner door came the irregular sound of typing. Uneasily I crossed the main office and pushed open the door. The man who sat at the desk, wearing an old-fashioned eyeshade, broke off the clatter of the typewriter, which was about a 1902 vintage, as was the roll-top desk and the heavy swivel chair. It was difficult to judge his age. As he pulled off the eyeshade, I saw that his forehead was deeply furrowed and his skin was curiously gray, while there was a blue tinge to his lips. At first glance I knew that this was a very sick man.

He studied me, head on one side, and then he smiled. He had a delightful smile, and from that moment I loved him. "You must be Allan Drummond's young friend, Katherine Forbes, the girl who is determined to support herself and look after her young brother. Well, well, I certainly underestimated Allan."

Mr. Eakins had an impish sort of look that belied his precarious health or was determined to ignore it. "Before we go any farther, brace yourself. I can't afford to pay you a cent more than eighty dollars a week. But, if you want the job, I can let you and your brother live in the basement apartment rent-free. There's a living room, a couple of small bedrooms, a bath and kitchen. Furnished after a fashion. I don't know. Well, there it is."

"It sounds perfect!"

He laughed outright. "Now how do you expect to earn this gigantic stipend?"

What on earth had I been afraid of? "First, I'd oil the hinges on that outside door so people would think you want them to come in and not to stay out. Then I'd take down those old pictures and put up fresh ones. Then I'd do your typing and take telephone calls and messages and," I took a long breath, "someday maybe I could tell people about your tours. I bet I could make their mouths water, because that's the way I feel about them."

He chuckled and then gave the small dry cough I'd heard in people with a cardiac condition. "Well, now." He chuckled again. "Somehow you don't look like Atlas ready to carry the world on your shoulders, but maybe you could breathe life into the place yet. You can see for yourself that the business is on the skids. We can't compete with the big outfits. My son is now managing the last large tour we are going to attempt. The costs keep rising and people aren't buying this sort of vacation package any more. Not from us, anyhow."

"Then why don't you arrange little tours for people with

18

just a little money? Make it a personal business. Not a luxury cruise or one of those with every hour of the day planned but —oh, something they've always dreamed of." I squealed. "But that's it! Dreams for sale."

He wasn't smiling now. He watched me with a thoughtful expression. "That takes a young imagination. How old are you, Miss—Hell, I'm going to call you Kate!"

"Twenty-one and I'm very practical."

Again he gave me that long thoughtful look. On top of the high roll-top desk was a cabinet photograph of a young man with a devil-may-care face, a lurking smile in his eyes, head set jauntily. I recognized him as the one Allan had referred to disparagingly as The Playboy of the Western World, older but with the same unmistakable challenge in the carriage of his head that was not quite arrogance, not quite cockiness, but somewhere in between. As we talked, I found my eyes going back to the face in the picture.

"That's my son," Mr. Eakins said, observing the direction my eyes had taken. "That's Tommy. He's a fine boy." There was pride and love but a note of doubt in his voice. "All he needs is a steadying influence."

Already it was apparent that Mr. Eakins approved of me, not only because I was eager to work but because I was anxious to take on the responsibility of a younger brother. Apparently Allan had made a good sales talk, building up my practical, down-to-earth qualities, but if Mr. Eakins thought I was going to be a little mother to his Tommy, he was mistaken. Anyhow, I decided without any doubt at all, Tommy was not looking for a mother-substitute.

Automatically Mr. Eakins reached for a cigarette and then

dropped it into an overfilled ash tray and tossed the package after it. "Can't seem to remember they are forbidden," he grumbled.

I removed the big ash tray, dumped out the contents, and moved it to a battered table where it would be out of reach. Mr. Eakins gave his infectious chuckle. "You are probably going to rule me body and soul. You're the managing type if I ever saw it, but I guess I'm going to like it. Well, here's my proposition. A low-paid job that might—just might— lead eventually to foreign travel by conducting tours. And, of course, might not."

He laughed outright at my dazzled expression. "Nothing to it. All fun and games while you enjoy the scenery. Except that you're responsible for the passports and the belongings and the behavior and the luggage of all the members of the tour; you listen to their grievances, you let them loose on shore and they get lost or stray half a dozen times a day. You placate them and soothe them and, in extreme cases, you tell them where to head in. You apologize for foreign food and the bugs they pick up in strange lands and for the purchases on which they have been gypped. You sympathize because the poor dumb foreigners don't speak English. With luck you catch a few quick glances at a new country from the deck because you are too busy to go ashore. It's a dog's life and it takes stamina, determination—and youth."

"And it's fun," I concluded.

He shook his head. "Incorrigible." He went on, "Well, there's the apartment, such as it is, which would provide a shelter. Now this little brother of yours—"

"He's eleven, going on twelve, and he won't be a nuisance; that is—"

Mr. Eakins leaned back in his chair; that needed oiling too. "I have lots of time. Tell me the worst: delinquency, dope, vandalism, plays around with explosives—"

I laughed. "Nothing like that. He's really a good kid. And no trouble. That is—well, the thing is," I admitted in a burst of honesty, "Mike is the most curious human being I've ever known. Everything interests him, and once his curiosity is aroused, he digs in until he has satisfied it. But he won't bother you. Really he won't."

"A kind of bloodhound in the house. Sounds interesting, at any rate, and out of the ordinary, which I'd expect of a brother of yours."

Before I could decide whether this was meant as a compliment or otherwise, Mr. Eakins stood up. He was taller than I had realized and he seemed a trifle lopsided until I noticed that he held himself oddly to compensate for a greatly enlarged heart. "Well, let's get the worst over and take a look at that basement apartment. If you can survive that, you're hired, Kate. Come along."

II

My heart sank at first sight of that dark basement, with worn linoleum on the floor, no curtains on dusty windows, the stove rusty and the shower, behind stained curtains, filthy, with a sliver of dried soap in the dirty soapdish. There were two small bedrooms, little more than bunks, each with a narrow bed, each looking out on the dingy alley. There was a living room about the size of my bedroom at home, with a sagging couch, a round table holding a Tiffany lamp, and a couple of beaten-up chairs with the upholstery frayed, probably by mice. To add to this charming picture, there were bars on the front windows, half of which were below street level, so that all you could see were bodiless legs walking by.

Following my eyes, Mr. Eakins explained quickly, "You're right on the street here, you know, and anyone could force his way in. The bars will keep you perfectly safe." He added in a stronger, more assured voice, "Perfectly safe. Don't pay any attention to all you hear about crime in the Village. Well, of course, you might get a chain for the door and we'll put some patent locks on the bedroom windows so they can't be jimmied open. No harm in taking reasonable precautions. Or if you like animals, you might be able to get hold of a watchdog cheap, might even pick up one for nothing at the pound. Cheaper and safer than a gun."

He sounded disturbed; apparently he had not seen the basement for some time and he was afraid I would refuse to live there. And how I wanted to refuse! I couldn't bring Mike to a place like this after our bright and sunny little house—Mike, who loved sunshine and the out-of-doors and was accustomed to a big lawn and a safe residential street in which to play, so that he could chase after a ball without the risk of being run over. It wasn't fair to Mike.

Then I recalled that in a little over two weeks the monthly bills would begin to come in. I remembered how much I had paid at the supermarket last time I shopped. Allan would be able to salvage little from Dad's business; he had estimated that there would be just enough to carry us for three months and pay moving expenses. And heaven knew when he would be able to sell our shabby little house in an unfashionable neighborhood.

22

I took a long breath. "When can we move in?"

To my surprise Mr. Eakins gave me a hug. "Good girl! I'll help you. Tell me what you need and I'll keep the home fires burning until you are settled and ready to work."

We shook hands on it, though I was determined to accept no favors from Mr. Eakins, not because I didn't like him but because I didn't want to start with a burden of obligations. I went out into the March day. To add to the general misery, snow was falling, not soft, gentle snow but hard little pellets that bit into my cheeks and made my eyes water. At least it looked that way and no one knew I was crying.

I had planned to lunch with Allan at his apartment, and by the time I reached his building, there was no trace of tears. True, Allan occupied an apartment with a Riverside Drive address, but the entrance was on a side street and a view of the river could be obtained only by leaning precariously out of the kitchen window. The place was neatly arranged but Spartan, as though Allan had not spent a cent for comfort, let alone luxury.

He showed me around. "It takes a long time to get started, though bigger orders are coming in all the time, but you have to wait months for payment on consignment orders. Sometimes I think it will take me forever to get hold of some real money."

"You're young yet."

"But I haven't all that time," Allan said.

Like his room in our Red Bank house, there was little that was personal. I recognized the record player and was surprised to see how many books he had. But what surprised me most was the large cabinet photograph of me, which he must have removed from the house without telling me. It was flanked by a group of three ceramic figures: the one of Mother with that flurry of movement about her and her vivid face; one of a serene nun with a composed mouth and downcast eyes; and one of a girl with big hungry eyes and a greedy mouth. She was also, I might add in all fairness, very beautiful.

"They make an interesting contrast," Allan said. "How like your mother you are, Kate!" For a moment his hands rested lightly on my shoulders, without insistence. "Have you thought of me at all? Thought of marrying me, I mean?"

"Allan, I wish I could, but—"

He removed his hands. "Don't give it another thought. God knows I have no right to expect anyone to share my life while I have so little to offer." He changed the subject abruptly. "How did you make out with Eakins?"

"He's a darling. He's going to pay me eighty dollars a week and let us have a basement apartment in his building rent-free. Mike and I can manage just fine."

"What about Tommy?"

"He's out of the country somewhere, managing a cruise or a tour of some kind for his father."

Allan smiled. "That's all right then."

III

I was so frantically busy preparing to move, sorting out, packing, and discarding old things and getting the basement into livable shape that I made the adjustment to drastic change almost without being aware of it.

Allan, of course, was a tower of strength. He hired a cleaning woman to wash windows and scrub that basement

24

apartment until it sparkled, at least as much as an apartment sunk half underground can sparkle. He ripped up the linoleum and equipped the bedroom windows on the alley with burglar-proof patent locks, and he hung the yellow curtains I had brought from home as a substitute for sunlight, laid the carpet in the living room and put down bright scatter rugs in the bedrooms. I had brought slipcovers from home, shabby but at least an improvement on the worn upholstery. On the table under the lamp I set the ceramic figure of Mother, where her gaiety defied the gloom.

When Mike and I arrived, Allan was waiting to welcome us, and on the table was a vase of red tulips. "Brave and courageous like you," Allan said. "Anyhow they match your hair." He added, "It's all you've ever let me give you, and cheaper than the solitaire I was pricing."

I saw Mike look quickly from Allan to me and knew that he would welcome the marriage.

Within two weeks after Mike and I had settled in the basement apartment, Allan found a buyer for our house. It didn't bring in much, but if I could keep the money intact, it might pay most of Mike's college fees when the time came. And Mike, to my relief, was not only contented, he was ecstatic. He found the Village inexhaustible in its novelty; he enjoyed going to school where there were so many races of children, which was an education in itself; and, most important of all, he acquired a congenial friend.

Friendship is a curious thing. Some wise person once said that we don't make friends, we just recognize them. No two boys could have been more dissimilar than Mike Forbes and Joe Blanchard in background, in character, and in interests. Mike was the most completely extroverted person I ever

25

knew, with little patience for anything that was not practical.

Joe Blanchard lived next door, not in the apartment building but in one of those odd cul-de-sacs you often find in the Village. We went through the entrance of the apartment building, along a hallway, out into a garden and, beyond the garden, there was a big, sprawling, two-story house with one of the most dramatic living rooms I ever saw. It was two stories high, with bookcases that ran up to the ceiling, and little mahogany ladders hung on a rod to carry one across from shelf to shelf, even above the fireplace. On one side a circular staircase wound to the second floor. A skylight covered half the ceiling and under it Mr. Blanchard worked on his sculpture, for he was one of the few successful professional artists in the Village. His wife, better known as Biddy Winkler, was active in Off-Broadway theater.

The result of this marriage was Joe, a handsome, vague, dreamy youth who, even at twelve, was, in my personal opinion, the most confirmed liar I had ever encountered. Mike denied this; he said Joe told the truth, he simply dramatized things to make them more interesting, bigger than life-size.

"Someday," I warned him darkly, "that boy is going to cry wolf once too often."

Three

By the end of a couple of weeks I learned that Tommy was expected home in a few days; that his ship had already left its last port of call. Mr. Eakins's voice always warmed when he spoke of his son, but there was a lurking trouble in his manner. It became more and more apparent to me, because Mr. Eakins was as transparent as a child, that he saw in me the savior of his playboy son. I wasn't having any.

The afternoon before Tommy's ship was to dock, Mr. Eakins went up to his apartment earlier than usual to get the rest on which his doctor insisted. He had barely gone, when I heard the familiar creak of the hinges and a young man, wearing a light topcoat over what, even to my inexperienced eyes, was an expensive suit, a loud shirt and flamboyant necktie, brown hair worn rather long, came in and whistled when he saw me. Then he grinned.

"Well, well, how like our Tommy to keep the prettiest girl in town hidden away down here."

"I am Mr. Eakins's assistant. May I help you?"

He came to sit on the edge of my desk and hold out a

well-groomed hand, which I could hardly refuse. Then he put both hands over his eyes and shivered. "Brrr! Frost-bitten, and on the first day of spring too." He had a wide, laughing mouth and narrow eyes that summed me up as though I were on a butcher's counter. He was, in an unpleasant sort of way, a singularly good-looking man. "I'm Dan Summers, an old friend of Tommy's. How long have you adorned these premises?"

"Just a few weeks. Mr. Eakins isn't well, you know. Not at all well. He needs someone to keep the office open when he has to rest."

His brows arched at the seriousness in my voice. "No kidding! What's wrong?"

"His heart."

"Bad?"

I nodded, trying to swallow the lump in my throat. No one could know Mr. Eakins and not love him. "Very bad. You can see by the way he holds himself that his heart must be terribly enlarged. I'm so worried about him that last week I almost cabled his son to fly home."

The visitor's jaw dropped. "Just who do you think you are kidding? Tommy is right here in town. I saw him myself a few nights ago at the Boul' Mich', that new hot spot in the Village, with," he paused slightly, "a luscious dame. Well, naturally it would be a luscious dame. You know our Tommy, always a perfect taste in women. Though cradle-snatching is something new for him. Like the Music Man, he usually seeks a more adult romance. If you know what I mean."

"I've never seen Tommy Eakins in my life," I said flatly. "He has been abroad for weeks, touring the Greek Islands, and his ship won't dock until tomorrow morning."

He scratched his head, watching me as though trying to catch me off guard. "There's something damned smoky going on or else Tommy has a double and, what's more, a double who is playing around with Tommy's girl."

"If you don't believe me, you can ask his father."

Dan Summers ran a finger across his lips and then leaned forward to ruffle my red hair. "Okay, maybe I was mistaken. Sorry if I got out of line on a misapprehension. If I did, you tell him I'll try to set it right. So we start over with the idea that he is not in New York, he wasn't out with a luscious dame, and he has never set eyes on you. Well, he has a treat in store, but you might tell him that, for once, Dan Summers saw you first. And, speaking of that, starting in the way I mean to go on, how about having a drink with me when you get through here?"

I refused, though I had had no dates since I had come to New York. Allan had left me strictly alone after that one lunch at his apartment. In a way I was sorry, but I knew that he was wise. But, lonely or not, I had no desire to go out with Dan Summers. He was as good-looking a man as I'd seen in a long time, but I didn't like him at all. I didn't like his bold eyes and assured manner. I didn't think he had any interest in me as a person but, whether, from sheer malice, he wanted to cut Tommy out or he wanted to get information from me, I did not know. Prosperous as he appeared to be, I was convinced that whatever dealings Dan Summers had would be to some extent dishonest.

He took my refusal with more amusement than disappointment and I had the feeling that he believed he had made a terrific impression. Again he ruffled my hair.

29

"You could practically warm your hands on a red thatch like that," he said, and flipped me lightly on the cheek. "Tell Tommy that Dan Summers was looking for him. If there's been any mistake, he had better get in touch with me at once. It's important." He gave me that wide grin in which there was no genuine mirth. "But he'll know that."

II

I had volunteered to work Saturday morning so that Mr. Eakins could be free to spend the time with his son, whose ship was to dock early. When I opened the office, he had not yet come down. This morning there were more telephone calls than usual, mostly from women wanting to know when Tommy would be home, and there were a number of routine letters to answer and bills to pay. I wondered, a little bleakly, how much longer Mike and I would be able to occupy, rent-free, the apartment that had already become home to us.

I was hard at work when the creak of the hinges brought my eyes up from the typewriter keyboard and I saw the man who stood looking around him in a diffident sort of way as though hesitating to intrude.

"What may I do for you?"

"I want to see Tommy." It wasn't diffidence; unless my imagination was running away with me, it was a kind of dread, almost fear.

"His ship has probably docked by now, but I don't expect him for a couple of hours; he'd probably be the last to leave his group."

The man was startled, unbelieving. "Tommy's been out of the country? That's what—but he was seen the other evening." The man came closer to my desk and his expression was unexpectedly formidable. "Let's not have any games. I want to see Tommy and I want to see him now. If you're afraid to disturb his beauty rest—and he probably doesn't get up until noon—I'll do it for you. Glad to."

"Well, he's not here; that's for sure, and he hasn't been here. I don't see how you can reach him at the dock, but you are free to try. He's coming in at pier—" I checked it and found the number at which the ship could be reached. Then I pushed the telephone within reach of his hand and saw then, in surprise, that although he was dressed in exquisitely tailored clothes, he wore a ring with a massive scarab in it, which provided a jarring note, completely out of character with the essential sobriety of the man.

He did not touch the telephone, but he sat down slowly in the chair beside my desk, like a balloon that had been deflated. "You are positive that Tommy has been out of the country?"

"He's been managing a tour of the Greek Islands, a big affair with over a hundred people. If someone thinks he saw him in New York, he must have a double. I understand most people do."

"A double? I suppose it's possible, but it's unlikely. Tommy is *sui generis,* as you know."

"I've never laid eyes on him." My manner was unnecessarily tart, but I was weary of the assumption that Tommy Eakins had only to look at a girl and she'd fall at his feet.

He started to get up and then settled back again. "I'd almost forgotten that this is a travel agency. Well, as long as I'm here, I might as well get some value out of it. I'd like to have a honeymoon cruise arranged, with no word leaking out

31

to the press. I'm just married and want a completely confidential job done. As an old friend, Tommy is the best one to handle it for me."

Old friends. I recognized him then. He was the third man in Allan's picture. This worried-looking man beside my desk was Fillmore Hatfield III, The Man Who Has Everything. He had an ageless sort of face, somewhat withered, and an awkward body beautifully groomed and tailored. A rather fine forehead and an ominously weak chin, with an unexpectedly sensual mouth. A corner of the mouth twitched. Twitched. He put up a manicured finger to steady it. He looked, I thought, as though he were recovering from a serious illness. Or as though he were afraid. One thing was obvious. Mr. Hatfield had steeled himself for an encounter with Tommy and he was taken aback, deflated at finding me. At last he cleared his throat with a rasping sound.

"Because of my—uh—position, there is too much publicity about what I do. My wife and I—uh—decided that the best way to avoid the press was to marry secretly and not inform anyone until after our return from our honeymoon. Because of the hasty marriage there have been no arrangements. I don't know whether you have ever been dogged by newsmen and cameras and microphones—"

I laughed and shook my head.

"You don't know how lucky you are. Well, Luisa and I are holed up at the Waldorf, because no one is likely to know us there and I can't trust the staff at my apartment to be above accepting bribes. We're living under a false name. Of course the management knows," he added hastily. "There is nothing irregular."

I stifled a giggle. Poor Fillmore Hatfield III had probably

never done anything irregular in his life, never sowed so much as one wild oat.

"Well, naturally that's no honeymoon for a girl like Luisa. I wanted something—uh—glamorous, but we married so hastily—and, in short, as long as I am here, I might as well get something out of it."

In spite of Hatfield's self-effacing air, I got the impression that it was his practice to "get something out of it."

"Perhaps you can fix up something attractive, without any publicity, so we can leave in a couple of days. The sooner, the better. If I take my yacht or plane, there is always someone in the media," he sounded as though he distrusted the media as much as President Nixon, "to find out, so if you can arrange a cruise to the Bahamas, the West Indies, even South America, I'd be grateful. Luisa rather thought of Monaco, but I—uh—have met the Prince and Princess, so perhaps—"

As he talked, he gained confidence, but I still had the curious impression that he was improvising as he went along, not about the secret marriage or the need for privacy, that part rang with unmistakable truth, but that was not what he had come to the agency to discuss with Tommy.

"Mr. Eakins will probably be down soon. I've been expecting him every minute. He'll surely be able to think of something Mrs. Hatfield will love."

His expression changed, some of the strain that had marked it seemed to relax, making him appear younger. He reached automatically for his billfold. Fillmore Hatfield III was accustomed to paying for what he got. Somehow I hoped that his Luisa did not care for money. Not too much, at least. And yet, if it wasn't money, I couldn't fit The Man Who Has Everything into a romantic context to save my life. I shook my head as he produced a bulging billfold. It had always been my understanding that men of great wealth rarely carried much money about with them, but I supposed that Hatfield needed the tangible assurance of its presence.

"Just to show my appreciation," he said, again with the diffidence that was strange in a man whose money was so formidable a power.

It wasn't until he reached the door that my slow wits caught up with me. "Mr. Hatfield!"

He turned abruptly, as though startled.

"You don't need to go to all this trouble to get privacy," I blurted out. "You can buy all you want. Why are you really trying to sneak out of the country this way?" And then too late I covered my mouth with my hand and stared at him, aghast. "Oh, I'm sorry. I had no right—I didn't know I was going to say that. Please forgive me."

He came back slowly, resumed his chair beside my desk. "I've got to get out of the country," he said flatly. "My life has been threatened."

"I suppose, having all that money—"

"Somehow, I doubt if it's the money," he said so seriously that I nearly laughed.

"What do the police think?"

"I haven't talked to them."

"Well, why not, for heaven's sake?"

"Because I thought I knew who was behind this and that I could handle it myself, which I'd prefer to do. Now I am at a loss." He straightened himself, the scarab ring flashing as he moved. "Anyhow," he said in a decisive tone, "I want to get away now with my wife."

34

"But it—whatever it is—will be waiting for you when you come home."

"That's a chance I have to take."

"If I were in your shoes, I'd run screaming to the police."

"Luisa wouldn't like that. She wouldn't like that at all. You can reach me as soon as you have anything mapped out —and make it urgent, please—at the Waldorf. Ask for Mr. Hyde. Mr. J. Hyde. Hurry it up, will you? Luisa is bored to death and you can't blame her; she's used to such a lively time." He nodded and went out.

Just married and already bored to death!

"Well," I said aloud to the empty office, and expelled a long breath. "Well!"

Obviously the rabbitlike Fillmore Hatfield was in a tizzy and, whether it was justified or just part of the man's makeup, something had to be done. This was more than I could cope with.

I didn't call Mr. Eakins in his apartment because the sound of the bell, if he was still asleep, might startle him. Some time before, he had given me a key to his apartment because he had accidentally locked himself out. I had never used it, never been on the second floor. Now I ran up the uncarpeted stairs and tapped lightly. When there was no reply, I tapped louder. Then I unlocked the door and eased it open, peering around it cautiously in case Mr. Eakins was wandering around undressed.

But he was dressed, except for his jacket, and lying on the couch with the reading lamp still burning, yesterday's newspaper lying on top of him.

Even before I reached the couch, I knew that he was dead. There is something about death you can't mistake, though I had never seen it before. Mike and I had not been permitted to see our parents; a kindly policeman had said he knew we'd be happier to remember them as they had been and he was sure that was what they would have preferred.

I knelt down and touched the cold hand that was lying with the fingers touching the carpet. The hand was already stiff. He must have been dead for hours, but at least he had died quietly, perhaps not even knowing what was happening to him. There had been no struggle, only a moment when his attention had wandered away from the paper, somewhere, nowhere.

I had truly loved him but I felt no real grief. This moment had awaited me from the day when I had taken the job. My only regret was that his son had not been with him at the last. I still held that cold, stiff hand in mine. Then I noticed that his fingers clutched a scrap of newsprint. It was part of some dull economic report, without beginning or end. I turned it over and read the brief item:

Eakins Travel Agency bankrupt. The agency, founded by Thomas A. Eakins in 1963, has joined the long list of small businesses that have been unable to survive the current recession.

I didn't believe it. Even then, I didn't believe it. Mr. Eakins would have told me. I knew that as surely as I knew anything. There was no plan in my mind. I tucked the piece of paper inside my bra. Then I went to the telephone, dialed, and said, "I want a policeman."

Knowing that the cruise ship must have docked by now, I found the proper number, but I had some difficulty in getting hold of anyone in charge of the tour. At last I got an impatient man who said, "Make it fast. We're busy."

"I've got to speak to Mr. Thomas Eakins."

"Sorry, but he's tied up."

"Then please get word to him that I have bad news for him. His father died last night. He must come home at once."

There was a pause and then the impatient man said, "My God! I don't know—Hey, who is this speaking?"

"Mr. Eakins's assistant. I've already called the police, but his son will have to take charge and make the arrangements."

"You've called the police? Why? Nothing odd about the old man's death, is there?"

"Oh, no. Of course not. It was his heart and he had been expecting it. But I didn't know what else to do."

"I see. Oh, hell! This really puts the lid on. The point is that Tommy isn't here. He left the ship before we started home and flew back on urgent personal business. I was supposed to cover for him, but we didn't expect anything like this. If he isn't home, I don't know where you can reach him, and that's a fact."

"Never mind." I set down the phone and stared out of the window, trying to understand what had happened. Evidently Summers had not been mistaken in thinking he had seen Tommy in New York, but he had not come home, he had not tried to get in touch with his father. Or—and I looked at the still figure on the couch—had he come home last night?

There was one thing sure. Tommy Eakins was going to

have a grim homecoming, with his father's death, Summers issuing enigmatic warnings, and Hatfield ready to confront him as an enemy, for apparently he believed, rightly or wrongly, that Tommy was responsible for the threats on his life. At least he had done so until I had convinced him that Tommy was out of the country.

I sat beside the couch until the police came, and they were very quick, only minutes after I had terminated my call to the ship. They were young men who patrolled this section regularly, and they, or at least one of them, had known Mr. Eakins, and, of course, had liked him.

I told them how I had happened to find his body and explained that he had had a bad heart and had known that he might die at any time.

The man who had known him, named Hennessey, nodded. "Yeah, he mentioned it to me once. Some hoods slashed my tires right outside the building on one of those bitter winter days, and darned if he didn't come out with some hot coffee and we got chinning. My old man had a bad heart and went just like this and we talked about it. He was a real nice guy. What family does he have?" And the policeman looked around the room, which obviously lacked any woman's touch.

"Only one son, so far as I know. I've worked here just a few weeks."

"Have you notified the son?"

"He's been managing a cruise among the Greek Islands ever since I've been here, so I've never seen him. But his ship docked this morning and I got word to someone on board." I don't know why I lied about it except that to protect his son was a way of keeping faith with Mr. Eakins and the last thing I could do for him.

"I'll report a D.O.A. on the car radio," the nice policeman said, and suggested that I return to the office. Nothing I could do here and I might as well get on with the job. Just what the old man would have wanted me to do.

So I went down to my desk and waited, and after a time an ambulance came and two young men went lightly up the stairs. I did not look out when they returned, walking more heavily. The man from the patrol car looked in to say that the son was to call a certain number and ask for a certain man as soon as he showed up.

And then everyone was gone and the building was empty and still. Even the street, for the moment, was without the usual sounds of traffic: screaming children, footsteps, radios and televisions going full blast. And in the silence I could hear from a record player the last movement of Beethoven's Ninth, the voices soaring in their triumphal "All men will be brothers," and I put my arms on my typewriter, and my head on my arms, and wept.

The hinges creaked and I looked up, wiping my cheeks with the backs of my hands, as the door opened, and stared at the tall young man who stood there, brows raised in a question, a half smile lurking in his eyes, head held jauntily. Here at last was Tommy Eakins, The Playboy of the Western World.

Four

He came forward and leaned over my desk, smiling, saw the tears still squeezing out of my eyes in spite of my effort to stop them, and his smile faded.

"Here," he said, and his voice was gentle; he certainly had a way with women, "what's wrong?"

I blew my nose and wiped my eyes.

"I am Tommy Eakins. You must be helping out my father." He talked easily, giving me time to regain my self-control. "And here I've been worrying about him when, if I had known he had someone like you to look after him—"

"I couldn't look after him," I wailed. "He's dead. He—"

I couldn't have been mistaken about the stunned shock in his face. The color faded even from his lips. "Dad? Dead? When—did it happen?"

"Last night. At least it must have been then. I found him this morning. He didn't come down and there was something I couldn't handle alone, so I went up and—he was there—on the couch. The reading lamp was still on and he hadn't undressed and he had been reading the paper."

As Tommy turned toward the door, I said hastily, "He's not there. He—I called the police and they've taken him away. You're to call this number; here's the man's name." "I—see." He sat down beside my desk and stared blindly at the window. At last, seeing that he was not going to talk, that he was just sitting there, I put into his hand the paper with the telephone number the police had left with me. And when he still didn't move, I pushed the telephone within his reach.

He roused himself then, dialed the number, asked for the man whose name I had been given, and introduced himself. Mostly he listened, saying, "Yes, I understand . . . I see. Okay, I'll take care of it . . . Yes, his physician is—was Dr. Phineas Clark. I don't know his address, somewhere in the Village . . . When can I see him? . . . No, I mean my father. . . . I see. Sorry, but this has been a shock to me . . . Oh, yes, I knew his health was precarious, but I guess we're never really prepared. . . . I got in just a few minutes ago from a cruise I've been managing for the firm. The Greek Islands . . . Thank you very much. I appreciate your help."

II

From upstairs I could hear the beat of restless feet as Tommy paced up and down the living room. There was no reason to believe that he would come back and that I would be needed, but I stayed on. Once I went into Mr. Eakins's office and saw, scrawled on the day's calendar, the word TOMMY. For a long time I looked at the picture on top of the desk. Then, as though I had no business to be there, I returned to my own office. There was nothing to do but I waited, not knowing for what I waited. Once I thought uneasily that I should go down and prepare Mike's lunch because on weekends I made sure he had a hot meal to compensate for the sandwiches he carried to school the rest of the time. But still I did not move.

When he appeared in the doorway, I knew that I had been waiting for Tommy. He looked haggard, but when he saw me, he smiled. "I was afraid you had gone, but I hoped you'd be here." He looked at his watch. "Half-past one. Have you had anything to eat?"

I shook my head.

"Then we'll go out to lunch." As he saw the protest in my face, he said, "We've got to have food, you know. We can't face—anything if we aren't up to par. And I want to talk to you about Dad."

"I can't go out. I must get lunch for Mike."

"Mike?"

"My little brother. We live down in the basement, you know."

"You live—*where?*"

"In the basement. Your father let us have it rent-free on account of he couldn't pay much salary."

Tommy was appalled. "You mean a kid like you is looking after a younger brother and living in the basement on what Dad could pay you?"

I nodded. "And I'm not a kid. Twenty-one, nearly twenty-two."

"How did you happen to make that kind of arrangement?"

"Well, really, I owe it to Allan Drummond. He thought it up when my parents died."

"Allan!" Tommy shook his head as though trying to clear it. "Allan saw you first and then let you go?"

"Well, this was sort of expedient, and Allan isn't making much yet." What I meant to imply, of course, was that Allan could not afford to hire me, but Tommy obviously misunderstood.

"I—see."

I covered the typewriter. "Do you—that is, shall I come to work on Monday?"

"Of course. Meanwhile," and he took my arm firmly, "we haven't settled that business about lunch."

"I'd like to, but I really meant it about Mike, Mr. Eakins."

"Tommy. Well, then, can't you add some water to the soup, or something?"

So I led the way down to the basement, calling, "Mike!" though I knew from the silence that he wasn't home. Mike couldn't seem to do anything without a background of music from a transistor radio, a Christmas present, which I frequently regretted.

"Oh, I forgot. He is going to have lunch and spend the afternoon with his best friend, who got a German police dog for a birthday present. I sent him off as clean as a pin in a brand-new green sweater I knitted for him, but I suppose by night he'll be a grubby little pig."

"And quite proper too." Tommy looked around the room and whistled. "You've made a nice job of this. Turned a slum into a bright little room. You're quite a girl. What's your name, anyhow?"

"Katherine Forbes."

"Kate," he said promptly, as his father had done. He wandered around and then picked up the little ceramic portrait of Mother. He smiled. "Whoever did that caught you just right, didn't he? That is, you must be like that, naturally

43

gay, when you aren't so subdued."

"That's not me. That's my mother."

He took it to the light from the barred windows, pushing aside the yellow curtains so he could study it more closely.

"I know that workmanship. Now who—oh, Allan, of course."

"Yes, Allan. Without him I can't imagine how Mike and I would have managed." I tied on an apron and got out the vegetable soup I had started the day before and put it on the stove. "There isn't much, some homemade soup and enough leftover pot roast for hot beef sandwiches. And coffee, if you want some."

"Perfect. Let me help. I haven't tasted home cooking for years."

"Nothing you can do." While I added some celery salt and parsley to the soup, we talked idly. He seemed more relaxed, though his color was still bad.

We ate lunch almost in silence. Now and then I looked up to find him studying me, a curious expression on his face. Now and then his thoughts were so far away that I knew he was unaware of my presence. But even when we had finished lunch and I had cleared away the dishes, Tommy sat on at the table.

"Tell me about Dad," he said abruptly.

"About—finding him?"

"No, everything. How you met him and got the job. The works. You liked him, didn't you?"

"I loved him."

He nodded. "Of course."

So I told him about the death of my parents and that I had needed a job immediately if Mike and I were to stay together

44

and make some kind of home, and how Allan Drummond as usual had come to the rescue, helped with all the details of the police, the funeral, disposed of Dad's business, sold the little house in Red Bank, and found me this job.

Again Tommy picked up the gay little ceramic figure. "You mean to tell me that Allan lived in the same house with you for three years and then let you go?"

"When he first asked me to marry him, I thought he was just being kind."

Tommy snorted.

"Well," I said indignantly, "Allan isn't like you. He doesn't make passes at every girl he meets."

Tommy's eyebrows arched in surprise. "My reputation, Iago. Oh, my reputation! And where did you pick up that nonsense?"

"Well, everyone—"

His eyes weren't smiling now. "Everyone?"

"Allan called you The Playboy of the Western World and said he wouldn't let me work here if you were around; and Dan Summers said something about you and your women and keeping me hidden away in the office while you were at the Boul' Mich' with a luscious dame."

"Oh, hell! Hell! Hell!" Tommy's fist crashed on the table, making the little ceramic figure leap. "Of all the filthy luck! A chance in a million and it would be Dan who saw us. That rat just comes out of cracks." He pulled himself together. "And where," he demanded, "did you come across Dan Summers? If you've got the sense of a day-old chick, you'll stay away from him. He's bad medicine to little girls."

"That's what he said about you," I retorted.

Unexpectedly Tommy grinned. "Temper! Temper! I

45

should have been warned by the red hair. But just the same you watch out for that heel."

"You're the one who had better watch out." I don't know, or perhaps I do, why I was so belligerent. "He came here yesterday to see you and he wouldn't believe me when I said you had gone on a cruise."

"Yes, I gathered that," Tommy said grimly.

"But when I tried to assure him that he was mistaken, that I'd never laid eyes on you, and you were on a ship that would dock this morning, I think he believed me. He said if he'd made a mistake, he'd try to set it right. Something like that. And he said to get in touch; it was important, very important, and you would understand."

"Set it right," Tommy repeated, frowning. "If he's been up to anything, I'll take him apart. I've about had it from friend Dan. Did you give my father his message?"

"No, I didn't."

"Why not?"

"I didn't like Summers any more than he likes you. And I didn't believe him then. I thought you really were on that ship."

Tommy's face did not change, but I moved farther back in my chair. "So you don't think so now?"

"I called the ship as soon as I found your father. I got hold of a man who said you'd flown home a week ago, and he was supposed to cover for you, but, of course, you hadn't expected anything like this."

"No, we didn't expect anything like this." Tommy fell silent, his long fingers drumming on the table until he became aware of it and thrust them into his pockets. "What made you go up to see my father this morning?"

"That was because of another friend of yours."

"Get this straight, youngster, and don't forget it. Dan Summers is no friend of mine. Nothing would give him more pleasure than to stab me in the back, and, if I understand correctly the message he left with you, that is just what he is trying to do or, God help us all, has already done."

"I didn't mean Summers. I mean Mr. Hatfield. I thought you were old friends because Allan has a picture of the three of you, taken on a Hawaiian vacation Mr. Hatfield paid for."

"And never let us forget."

"Yes, I sort of gathered from Allan that the friendship, on his part at least, had soured, because I asked him if a man like Mr. Hatfield, with so many businesses, couldn't find a job for me in one of them. But Allan wouldn't ask him. He said he wouldn't take anything more from him."

"How wise he was! Fillmore Hatfield practically makes a career out of what he frequently refers to as his 'little private charities,' but I never heard of one that didn't have a string attached. I suppose it's the only way he has of making his personality felt, which normally has all the impact of a slack rubber band. Well," Tommy's hands came out of his pockets and his fingers drummed again on the table, "what did Fillmore want?"

"He was looking for you, almost as though he were trying to confront you. He was stunned when I told him you weren't here, that your ship hadn't docked yet. At first he refused to believe me because someone had seen you—"

"Dan! Yes, that's what I figured."

"Well, Mr. Hatfield had got this idea you had been in New York for the past week and though he'd been told that it might be a mistake, he didn't believe me."

Tommy's fingers were motionless now, rigid.

"Well, when he finally believed me, he said something like, as long as he was here anyhow perhaps he could get some use out of it. He wanted the agency to arrange for a honeymoon cruise for him right away." I repeated Mr. Hatfield's reasons for wanting to get away without publicity after his hasty and secret marriage. "He's in a tearing hurry. He wants to leave town at the first possible moment. And he said your father could reach him at the Waldorf under the name of Hyde. J. Hyde."

A reluctant grin twisted Tommy's mouth. "Jekyll and Hyde. He would think of that. But the Waldorf! That's not Fillmore's kind of place. I suppose he had his eye on all those convenient exits."

"He said both he and his wife disliked publicity. What's so funny about that?"

"Go on."

"I didn't know how to handle it alone and there was a hurry about it, so I went up to consult your father and—found him." My voice trailed off.

Tommy was watching me intently. At the moment he did not look at all like a playboy. "What are you holding back as grimly as the boy with the wolf under his cloak?"

"I always wondered how he managed that."

"Go on, Kate; don't keep me in suspense."

"Well, I don't want to sound like Joe."

"Who is this new character you are introducing into our stirring drama?" Tommy's words were light but not his expression.

"He's a friend of my little brother and he makes things up,

or at least he dramatizes them until you never know how much is real and how much is make-believe."

"Okay, let's have it; dramatized or not."

"Well, I think Mr. Hatfield was taken aback when he saw me."

"So was I." And for once Tommy's smile was genuine. I ignored that. With Tommy you learned quickly, in self-preservation, how much to ignore. "I didn't believe—that is, I believed the part about the secret marriage and the fact he wanted to get away, but I don't think he intended to tell me about it when he came in. It was just sort of spur of the moment. And he was—I thought he was sort of girded up to meet you as though he expected trouble. And he was afraid."

"Hey!" Tommy protested. "Afraid of me?"

"Well, I asked what he was afraid of and he said his life had been threatened and he thought he knew who was doing it, but now he wasn't sure. So it must have been you. And he wouldn't go to the police because his wife wouldn't like it."

"That's for sure."

"Oh, you know her?"

"All I want to." His fingers were drumming again and once more he thrust them into his pockets, annoyed by his self-betrayal. At last he reached for a cigarette case in which there was only one cigarette. He offered it to me and I shook my head. "Good," he said, and once more his smile was unforced. "I've cut down to three a day and that's the last one left."

He lighted it, inhaling deeply, enjoying the sensation of the smoke drawn into his lungs, as people do when they are breaking a habit that, for all its dangers, has been a pleasant experience.

"I decided to cut out smoking when Dad had to, because it was only an added aggravation to him and anyhow any smoke in the room was potentially dangerous for a heart requiring oxygen. Now I suppose—no, I've got this far. Might as well finish the process. The worst is over. Now have I got it all or are you holding out anything?"

"Not a thing," I said indignantly. "Well, that is—"

He laughed. "All right. Tell me the worst."

"It's probably nothing at all." I fumbled inside the neck of my dress and drew out the scrap of newsprint. "This was in your father's hand when I found him."

Tommy read it in disbelief. "But it's not true! It can't be true. Dad would never have taken a step like that without consulting me, and anyhow we aren't that close to the shoals. I've been figuring that we can keep afloat for a long time if we don't try for the big stuff."

"I didn't believe it either. But, oh, Tommy, suppose he saw this and it caused the shock that brought about his fatal heart attack."

With an ejaculation Tommy scraped back his chair and went to my telephone. "All right if I use this?" He flipped pages in the huge Manhattan directory, called a newspaper office, got the financial department, and talked to a stand-in for the financial editor, for Saturday is without important news because the stock market is closed, and the bulk of the Sunday financial section is already running through the presses.

When he put down the phone, he was frowning. "He doesn't know where the item came from and he can't reach his boss who is in Washington trying to get straight stuff on market futures. Some people never give up hope."

All of a sudden there was an uproar in the alley. Usually the only sounds were when the garbage cans from the restaurant at the other end of the alley were rolled out to the street to be emptied, or when there was a cat fight or the rattle of garbage can lids when rats were prowling.

A woman screamed and then there were running feet and a man shouting. In almost no time a small crowd had gathered at the street end of the alley. In New York people seem to come out of the pavement when there is any kind of excitement.

I ran into my bedroom, followed by Tommy. Half a dozen people were milling around, gesticulating, shouting in a confused way, but I could see nothing except for a few garbage cans with their lids tossed on rakishly and a huddle of people looking down. A siren wailed and then policemen were running—the same men who had come in answer to my call earlier in the day about Mr. Eakins.

Tommy managed the intricate lock, flung open the window, and leaned far out. "Good God! There's a man down there. I can't make out whether he's drunk or hurt."

One of the policemen had driven back the crowd while the other returned to the radio car to call in and report. And before long there were more sirens and blinking lights and men converging on the alley: a doctor with a bag, men with cameras and other equipment. The crowd had drawn back but still watched, silent.

Then a long basket was hauled out of an ambulance and Tommy said sharply, "The man must be dead. This is no place for you."

Obediently I turned around and headed back for the living room, but Tommy did not follow me. The waiting crowd had moved aside, or been pushed aside, to make way for stretcher bearers, and Tommy was staring, rigid, white-faced. For a moment I thought he was going to be sick, but it may have been the poor light from the alley, for when he joined me, I thought I must have imagined the fleeting expression on his face, which had drained all the youth and gaiety out of it, leaving it hard and remote.

"Thank heavens Mike isn't here!" I exclaimed.

"He'd probably enjoy it," Tommy said dryly. "All twelve-year-olds are ghouls at heart."

"He's only eleven," I said, and then realized how silly I sounded. The finding of that dead man in the alley had shaken me badly.

Tommy checked his watch. "Four o'clock. I've kept you all afternoon." He smiled down at me. "I'm glad my father had you with him those last weeks, Kate. Very glad." He started toward the door, turned back. "When you told the police I wasn't on the ship—"

"I didn't tell them."

"Why not?"

"I don't know why," I said in a small voice.

A moment later I heard him running lightly up the steps of the agency. Only then did I realize that, in all that long conversation, I had been the one to do the talking. I still didn't know where Tommy had been during the week when he was supposed to be on the cruise ship.

Five

Even after the body had been removed, the crowd lingered in the alley. The doctor and the cameramen and most of the police had gone, but several remained, questioning the people who hovered, watching, though there was nothing to see now. One of them glanced at the window where I stood, half concealed behind the curtain, and after a while there was a tap at the door.

"You're—ah—Miss Forbes, the young lady who called us this morning about Mr. Eakins." He added, "This seems to be your day for finding bodies."

"I didn't find the one in the alley! I never knew anything about it until a woman screamed and people began to shout. What happened to him?"

"He was murdered," Hennessey said.

"Out there?"

"Must have been. No one is likely to carry a dead body around the streets. Sure you didn't hear anything?"

"Just what I told you."

53

"How long have you been down here? You sure had a box seat."

I thought back. "I stayed in the agency office until a little after one-thirty; then I came down and got lunch and I've been here ever since." For some reason I did not mention Tommy.

"According to the Doc, he had been dead quite a few hours; they'll get the time down closer, of course, when they do the autopsy."

"Hours!" I was incredulous. "And no one noticed him in all that time?"

"He was lying behind a bunch of garbage cans and there isn't much light in the alley."

"Who was he?"

"He was clean." As I looked blank, Hennessey explained, "His pockets were empty, no identification, no keys, no bill-fold, not a scrap of paper. Nothing."

"That's the first mugging I've heard of since I moved to the Village. People around here, most of them anyhow, have so little money I suppose it is hardly worthwhile."

"Could be a mugging, of course," the other policeman said doubtfully. "Some of the hoods doing this kind of thing don't seem to care how much they get out of it, it's sheer sadism, a kind of hate, an outlet for brutality."

"Was he beaten up?"

For the first time he spoke sharply. "What makes you ask?"

"Because that's what happened to my parents, less than two months ago. They were robbed of less than three dollars and they would never have tried to fight back, but their skulls

54

were cracked." I set my teeth hard and willed myself not to cry.

"That's tough. Real tough. We get these things now and then. Yes, this guy was beaten savagely about the face and head; his face was just a pulp. His own mother wouldn't have recognized him. More like hate than silencing a victim before he could cry out." Hennessey looked around. "You live here all alone?"

"No, I have a little brother but, thank heaven, he's not here. He's at a birthday party."

"I see you have bars on the front windows and patent locks on the ones on the alley. Well, look out for yourself, Miss Forbes. There's a saying that deaths come in threes."

With these heartening words the men left and I scurried around, trying to catch up with my usual Saturday chores. I took the bedding and towels and Mike's shirts to the laundromat and did my week's shopping. I piled the heavy grocery bags and clean laundry in the two-wheeled cart that saved me so much carrying and went back to the apartment to put things away and do some basic cleaning.

The exertion was good for me and helped me to get my mind off the death of Mr. Eakins. It was dark now except for lights on street corners and in the windows of the apartment building next door. The basement apartment had never seemed so quiet. Now and then I heard the snarl of a cat fight in the alley and occasionally the lid on a garbage can was knocked over with a clatter by hungry rats or human predators.

Partly because I had so much to think of and partly because I had lunched later than usual, and so wasn't hungry,

I wasn't aware of how late it had grown. Then I noticed that it was seven-thirty. Occasionally the Blanchards kept Mike for dinner, but one or the other of them always called me first. Mr. Blanchard had assured me, when I said I hoped Mike wasn't being a nuisance, that his conversation had a peculiar fascination for him. The Blanchards were really awfully nice people.

When I had taken over responsibility for Mike, I had promised myself not to be a nagger; at least, any more than I could help. So I waited until eight-thirty before I called. It was Mr. Blanchard who answered. His wife, he explained, was out trying to raise some money for a new production.

"I think Mike has forgotten how late it is. Will you remind him, please, that it's time to come home?"

"Mike? He isn't here, Kate."

"When did he leave?"

"So far as I know he hasn't been here. I was up town most of the day arranging for a one-man show, but—hey, Joe, turn down that television set, will you? Have you seen Mike today?"

There was a murmur of voices and then I heard Mr. Blanchard say, "His sister is on the phone. I think you'd better talk to her."

Then there was Joe's rather shrill voice. "This is Joe speaking. Dad says you want to talk to me."

"I was asking about Mike. I thought he was planning to spend your birthday with you."

"Well, he was, but something came up and he couldn't make it."

"What came up? I don't understand this." There was panic in my voice.

56

"He called up—oh, about ten-thirty. He was all excited. He said something awful had happened and he didn't know how to handle it, but he'd have to do something. He tried to explain but he was so rattled I couldn't make out what was the matter and then he kind of yelped 'Joe, Joe!' and he rang off in a hurry."

"This was at ten-thirty this morning?"

"About then. I didn't check. But he'd planned to come at ten, so I'd been sort of looking out for him for quite a while. We were going together to see about dog training for Wolf, my police dog I got today. You know, obedience class. We were both going to take it and sort of share Wolf, you know."

"And that's all Mike told you? Everything he said? Are you sure?"

"Well, part of it was sort of garbled, mixed up, you know, as though he was too excited to think straight. And his voice got high, the way it does. You know."

"I know." After a moment I said, "Look here, Joe, you aren't making this up, exaggerating, are you?"

He sounded aggrieved. "Oh, no, Kate. Honest."

Again there were background voices and then Mr. Blanchard said, "What seems to be wrong, Kate? I take it that Mike has turned up missing, but you know Mike. Apparently he is off on some ploy of his own."

"Yes, I know Mike. I'm sorry to have bothered you."

"No problem, and don't worry too much, my dear. Mike is a bright kid with a level head and as sure on his feet as a cat. But if you get anxious, give us a ring and Biddy or I will come over."

Mr. Blanchard was right, of course. Mike always landed on his feet. He couldn't get into any trouble, any real trouble.

There had been the time when he trailed the thief from Allan's shop. It might be something like that. It had to be something like that.

With all my will power I thrust out of my mind Joe's report of the conversation. Mike and something awful he had to handle, Mike babbling with uncontrolled excitement, Mike shut off abruptly. That was Joe all over. Dramatizing, distorting, making the most exciting account he could of it. If he was my son or younger brother, I'd cure him of his Baron Munchausen tales in five minutes flat and he'd eat standing up for a week. The more I thought of Joe, the angrier I got and, in a way, the more my anxiety about Mike was relieved. Unconsciously I was directing all my worry into a different channel.

But when the telephone rang at eleven-thirty, I leaped out of my chair and ran to answer it. Mr. Blanchard was calling, his voice full and assured and cheerful. "Biddy and I just wanted to make sure that all was well before we turn in for the night. Where had the little imp been? You tell him I'll tan his hide the next time he frightens his nice sister like that."

"He isn't here, Mr. Blanchard. He never came home. I haven't heard anything."

There was a silence and then Biddy Blanchard's light voice came over the telephone. "You poor child! I've dragged Joe over the coals, but he doesn't know a thing except what he made out of that scrambled call from Mike."

I'd been under a strain and now my irritation broke out. "What I can't understand is why Joe waited all day, waited until I called, to let me know that something was wrong with Mike."

"Well," Biddy said helplessly, "you know small boys. He seems to have assumed that Mike is off on some adventure. He's just reading *The Three Musketeers,*" she added as though that explained everything. "Would you like to have me come over for a while?"

"No," I said drearily, "I'm not afraid of being alone. I'm just afraid about Mike."

Then Mr. Blanchard broke in, and I realized they were speaking on separate phones. "You know, Kate, I think it would set your mind at rest if you called the police. Ask for the Missing Persons Bureau. It will take the responsibility off your shoulders. They're a good, efficient outfit, you know, and they'll turn him up for you before you know it."

So for the second time that day I called the police. The man on the phone was patient, kind, courteous, but he couldn't have cared less. He was not in the least concerned. There was just one idea in his head: Mike had gone away of his own free will. Lots of boys his age ran away at one time or another, and usually they turned up safe and sound.

Not Mike. I tried to explain about Mike. He was reliable, responsible. He wouldn't do that to me.

The policeman had heard all this a thousand times before, of course. "The night's young yet. Ten to one he'll show up."

"He's only eleven and he's never been out in the city alone at night. And something happened." I tried to explain Mike's frantic call to Joe.

The policeman wasn't impressed. "Have you had any discipline problems? Any arguments? Told him he couldn't do something he wanted?"

"Of course I have. Anyone looking after a small boy has to enforce discipline."

59

"Uh-huh. Well," as though yielding a point, "can you give us a description?"

I did so as accurately as I could, but the statistics—age, height, weight, color of hair and eyes, no scars or disfiguring marks—would fit a lot of small boys, not Mike, with his rough thatch of flaming red hair and his lopsided smile that charmed people, much to his disgust, as he had a low opinion of masculine charm.

"I'll tell you what," the policeman said cheerfully, "if the boy isn't home by morning, you drop in and we'll talk it over. Okay?"

"No," I said, my temper flaring, "it is not okay. Something has happened to my little brother and it's your job to find out what it is and make sure he is safe."

He sighed. "Do you know how many eleven-year-old boys there are in this city, just on Manhattan alone?"

"How many eleven-year-old boys have you?" I asked.

There was a short pause. "What do you expect us to do, Miss Forbes?" he asked in a reasonable tone. "What do you think has happened?"

"I think Mike saw something terribly wrong and tried to do something about it—something too big or too dangerous for him to handle alone. All I know for sure is that he is missing. He may be hurt. He may be dead."

"Kidnaped, perhaps?" And then I heard the amusement in the official voice.

"That's about the only thing I'm not afraid of. I couldn't raise enough money to get a dog out of a pound. No, it isn't kidnaping. But he might be injured. At least you must have a way of checking on hospitals, places like that, and if anything—happened—"

"The morgue."

"For God's sake, do something!"

It must have been about two o'clock when the sharp ring of the telephone jerked me out of the light doze into which I had fallen, curled up on the couch in a warm robe.

It was the same policeman. "Well," he said cheerfully, "we have good news for you."

"You've found Mike!"

"Well, no, but we can eliminate some possibilities. He isn't in any hospital."

"Is that—all?"

The anguish in my voice seemed to reach him then. "You said yourself that kidnaping is out. And murder? Well, it's not easy to get rid of a body and there are darned few motives strong enough for murdering a small boy. My guess is that he's just gone off for fun and that he'll show up in the morning."

So finally, at three o'clock, I rang Allan's number. He sounded wide-awake and alert and grasped the situation immediately. My last lurking hope was that Mike had gone up to see him, though common sense told me that Allan would have let me know.

"Steady," he said in his reassuring voice. "How long has Mike been gone?"

"I don't know exactly. He left a sort of garbled message with Joe Blanchard—but you know Joe. Well, of course, you don't. He—Joe exaggerates things, he distorts them. I never know how much is real and how much he dramatizes. He's always been that way. Biddy, his mother, told me that when he was just a toddler, he came running in with his eyes as big as saucers to say he'd been chased by a bear, when it was only a kitten."

"What have you done?"

I told him. "The police didn't take me seriously. They think Mike probably ran away from home to escape too severe discipline or just for the hell of it. But I made them check hospitals and at least I know he hasn't been hurt. Allan, I know I have no right calling you in the middle of the night, but I was frantic and you're the only one I have to turn to."

"Of course. That's what I'm here for." Allan considered for a moment. "There's really nothing very useful we can do tonight. Now I want you to take two of those sleeping pills the doctor gave you after your parents died. Don't worry for fear you won't wake up when Mike comes home. He'll see to that. In the morning I'll get hold of the Blanchard boy— give me the address, will you? . . . Oh, right next door. I'll find out what, if anything, he knows and we'll go on from there. What did you tell them at the Missing Persons Bureau? . . . All right, it's in my hands now, dear. Go to sleep."

"Oh, Allan!"

"Keep your fingers crossed," he said cheerfully. "Mike always wins through everything. Go—to—sleep."

And, believe it or not, with Allan's comforting voice like a reassuring handclasp, I went to bed without taking the pills and fell into a sound sleep.

II

I slept late, rousing only once when there was a loud argument in the alley about a missing garbage can. Someone was protesting shrilly, "I never touched it! What would I want with it?" Another voice shouted, "You won't get away with it. Twenty bucks apiece I paid for those cans, and I had my initials burned in them."

When I finally awakened, I showered and dressed, knowing that Allan would be coming at any time. It was strange not to hear the sound of Mike's penetrating whistle, always off pitch, or the clatter he made while he dressed. But somehow I felt sure this morning that Allan would cope, that he would find Mike and bring him safely home.

When he tapped at the door, I ran to meet him and he took me in his arms, holding me, rocking me as though I were a small child, and I rested my head gratefully against his shoulder.

"I'm so sorry," he said, his voice grave. "I'm so sorry." Then, more cheerfully, "Got any extra coffee? That smells good." When he was settled, with a cup of coffee on the table beside him, he said, "Now tell me about it. I assume you've had no further word this morning."

I shook my head. "And I know how busy you are. I had no right to disturb you, but you're the only one I could call."

"You could give me that right by a single word, Kate. I told you weeks ago I wanted you to marry me. I begged you. If we'd been married then, this need never have happened."

"Please don't, Allan. You're so terribly good and I make outrageous use of you, but I don't love you enough."

He smiled. "How do you know? I'm not a very enterprising lover, am I? Because you seem so young, I've never really tried to make love to you. Perhaps that was a mistake." Then his tone grew more serious. "We will forget all that. For now. But there's one thing: we belong together and someday you'll know that. I'm not going to hurry you, not with all this on your mind, not after the horrible day you must have spent."

"The worst day of my life!" I told him about finding Mr. Eakins's body, about having to break the news to Tommy, and the discovery late in the afternoon of the body of a murdered man in the alley. And then, on top of everything else, Mike had disappeared, leaving a queer, ominous message with his friend Joe Blanchard.

"I've just come from seeing Joe," Allan said. "Quite a place they have there, hidden back of that old apartment building. They must be well-heeled. Some people seem to make money easily and others, like me, don't make anything at all. Well, that's straying from the point. What a screwball Joe is! How much of that so-called telephone message did you believe, and how much did Joe make up out of whole cloth?"

"I don't know," I admitted helplessly. "I have never known how much to believe where Joe is concerned."

"Or whether there ever was a telephone message. The kid may have fabricated the whole thing."

"But why on earth would he do that?"

Allan shrugged. "God knows. He strikes me as one of those kids who believe more in their fantasies than in what really goes on around them. He had about a dozen theories to account for Mike's disappearance: he had witnessed a bank robbery, though there isn't a bank in the neighborhood; he was trailing a criminal; he had stumbled into a Commu-

64

nist plot and was being held as a hostage; and that was just a start. What it boils down to is that Joe doesn't have a clue as to what really happened, or why Mike was even around the apartment on a Saturday morning. I thought that was when he is supposed to help you with the shopping."

I explained the change in plans because of Tommy's expected return from a cruise that morning.

"You mean he actually was out of town! I must have misjudged him. Well, it's a cinch we can't get anything useful out of Joe."

"Mike has complete faith in him," I said. "He swears that the boy is truthful, but I've always said he'd cry wolf once too often."

"Personally," Allan said, "I don't believe he ever had a message from Mike. If the kid was really in trouble, he'd have called you or me, not a boy his own age who couldn't do anything about it."

I should have thought about that before. I could not hold down my tearing anxiety. "Allan, do you think Mike is in any real danger?"

Allan started to give me a reassuring answer and then he saw my expression. "I don't know. If there is any way I can save him, I'll do it. That's a promise. I'm fond of Mike, you know. I would be, even if it weren't for you." He pulled me to my feet. "Come along. We'll go put a burr under the saddle of that guy at the Missing Persons Bureau."

When Allan had introduced us both to the men at the Bureau, they were pleasant and courteous. But from the moment I began to speak, I knew it was no use. They were convinced that Mike had run away from home to escape what he regarded as unreasonably severe discipline. He was bound to turn up. He'd done this sort of thing before, hadn't he? They'd keep in touch. They smiled pleasantly at me and at Allan.

In the taxi on our way back to the apartment, Allan asked abruptly, "Look here, Kate, how are you going to manage now without—"

I kept my voice steady. "Without Mike?"

"Good Lord, I didn't mean that. He'll show up any time. No, I meant without a job now Mr. Eakins is dead. It must have been tough on you, finding him that way."

"It was. I truly loved him, Allan. He was one of the nicest people I have ever known, and the worst of it is that his death may have been brought about by shock."

"Shock?"

I told him about the news item announcing the bankruptcy of the travel agency, which had been clutched in his hand when I found him. "And it wasn't true. Someone did that deliberately."

Allan looked at me, frowning. "Oh, nonsense. That just couldn't happen."

"But it did happen."

"Okay, it did happen." Obviously, Allan was not interested. "But that does not answer my question. What are you going to do about a job and a place to live?"

"I still have my job. Tommy says I can stay on as long as I like."

"Tommy!"

"I know you don't like him, Allan, any more than you like that other old friend of yours, Fillmore Hatfield, the one you called The Man Who Has Everything, though if ever there was a misnomer, that's the one."

66

"How would you know? Or are you now moving among the Beautiful People?"

I told him about Mr. Hatfield coming to the agency to arrange for a secret honeymoon cruise and that he and his bride were living under assumed names because someone was threatening his life and he was scared silly.

Allan was incredulous. "Fillmore confided in you that he was afraid for his life? You know what, Kate, you are beginning to sound like Joe Blanchard. Watch out, girl! The Fillmores of this world do not patronize small-time agencies. They have secretaries who have other secretaries who work through underlings to handle these things for them."

"Actually," I blurted out, "he came to see Tommy and it was only as an afterthought that he asked us to fix up a cruise for him."

"To see Tommy," Allan said in an odd tone.

"Yes, and he could hardly believe that Tommy had been out of the country on a cruise. He was sure someone had seen him somewhere. And he really was scared out of his wits, Allan. That isn't make-believe."

"Such few wits as he ever possessed. This fascinates me. Tell me all. Just what did Flustered Fillmore have to say? The idea of his opening his shy heart to a total stranger boggles the imagination."

Allan listened in rapt interest while I described my interview with the multimillionaire. "Fillmore in a dither! But why did he want Tommy? Why, in the name of heaven, Tommy? He has no more use for Tommy than I have. The perennial playboy." Then he did a double-take. "He thought Tommy was in New York? Well, well, and I can guess what had him stirred up. I can make a good sound guess. Tommy has been trying for months to make time with Fillmore's girl."

"His wife," I corrected him. "Do you know her?"

"Barely acquainted, but somehow I thought Tommy was out of the running. Fillmore would provide stiff competition even for Tommy."

The taxi had stopped in front of the building, but Allan sat without moving, his thoughts apparently far away. "Just when did Tommy turn up?"

"In the late morning. About eleven-thirty. It was an awful shock to him because he thought a lot of his father and he was just too late. The police had already taken him away."

"Tommy is a very plausible guy. I doubt if he ever gave his father much thought."

"Mr. Eakins was crazy about him," I said defensively, but I remembered that note of doubt in his voice, his implication that Tommy needed a firm hand on the reins. I remembered, too, the man called Summers saying he had seen Tommy with a luscious dame at a Village hot spot the week before, but I didn't mention it to Allan. There was no point in stirring him up any farther.

Six

Sunday dragged by its interminable length. Waiting was hell. If anything had happened to Mike, if he had disappeared forever and I'd never see him again, never know what had become of him, I couldn't bear it. I remembered all the times I had been unreasonably short with him, the times I had refused him treats he had set his heart on, like going to the Music Hall or Yankee Stadium or taking the boat trip around the island, because we couldn't afford it. I kept thinking of that somber line of Edwin Arlington Robinson's: "We've each a darkling hill to climb." This was mine.

At every step I was alert, expecting to hear Mike come clattering down the stairs. At every ring of the telephone I hoped for good news. But it was always the same. The police called, but to ask for news rather than provide any. Biddy Blanchard called, expressed deep concern when I drearily repeated my "No news," and offered her services or those of her husband. There were several calls from boys I had dated in Red Bank, but they didn't ask me out any more. New York was too far and too expensive for their budgets, as most of them were either job-hunting or earning very little money.

I went over and over the events of Saturday, the most horrible day of my life, beginning with that curious encounter with the frightened Fillmore Hatfield, then the discovery that Mr. Eakins had died, and ending with the loss of Mike. Once I picked up the gay little figure of Mother, but I hardly dared look at it, knowing how I had failed with Mike, letting him go off into the unknown. Mike who had so much curiosity, so much intelligence, and so little knowledge of the world around him. I had sometimes complained about the amount of noise one small boy could make, but now I would have welcomed it. How I would have welcomed it!

On Sunday this section of the Village is almost as deserted as Wall Street. Once I heard the hinges creak as Tommy let himself out of the office and his legs went past my window. They paused as though he intended to come in, and then went on, walking swiftly, and I felt a pang of disappointment. It would, I explained to myself, be nice to have someone to talk to, something to break the stillness.

There hadn't been much time to think about Tommy, who had been somewhere in New York for the past week, a week of secret activities he had been unwilling to divulge even to his father. Tommy who was threatened by the man Summers. I wondered whether he had responded to Summers's peremptory demand to call him. Tommy whom Fillmore Hatfield had come to the agency to confront. Because of his bride, as Allan suggested? Had Tommy been playing around with Hatfield's wife and lost out because he did not have enough money to compete? It did not concern me in the least how many luscious dames Tommy Eakins had been seeing, and probably would continue to see.

Waiting is the most terrible thing there is. I couldn't read. I couldn't concentrate on anything. My mind was calling frantically, "Mike! Mike! Where are you? Let him be safe. Please. Please." Though I did not know to what I prayed.

Allan called, sounding exhausted, and I knew by his voice that he had learned nothing. "Anything new?"

"Nothing."

"What about his friend Joe? Has he heard anything?"

"Oh, how stupid I am! I never thought of that. I'll call right away, though I'm sure his parents would have known if he had heard anything."

"You can't be sure with a kid like that. See what you can find out and, if you hear anything, let me know. Otherwise we'll call it a day. Be sure to get yourself something to eat, Kate; you can't afford to break down."

I called Joe, but the Blanchard houseman said the family had gone out of town unexpectedly because of the illness of Mrs. Blanchard's aunt and they would probably be gone for several days.

I scrambled an egg and ate a piece of toast and felt better, more alert mentally, as I switched on the evening news and sat staring at the screen and an enlarged picture of Fillmore Hatfield III.

That morning, the announcer said, Mrs. Fillmore Hatfield, wife of the shy multimillionaire, had called the police to say that her husband had disappeared. They had just been married, a secret marriage to avoid publicity, and they had been living incognito at a midtown hotel. Mr. Hatfield had left his wife on Saturday morning on an unspecified errand —she had suspected that he intended to buy her a present of some sort—and she had not seen or heard from him since.

71

No trace of Mr. Hatfield had been found, though a six-state alarm had gone out. No ransom demand had been received from kidnapers, if this was a kidnaping. Mr. Hatfield was thirty years of age, five feet eight, weight 130 pounds. A narrow face, clean-shaven, light brown hair clipped short. When last seen, he was wearing a dark gray suit, blue shirt, and dark blue necktie. Anyone having any information . . .

II

Anyone having any information. But that meant me. Hatfield had come to the Eakins Travel Agency looking for Tommy. Then he had walked out and disappeared into thin air.

I went to the telephone, picked it up, put it down again. Twice yesterday I had called the police, once to report the death of Mr. Eakins, again to report that Mike was missing. A third call—I sat drumming my fingers uncertainly and thought of Tommy, who did that when he was upset. It was ridiculous to be afraid of the police. This was merely a coincidence, nothing more. But two missing persons from the same address! Or did lightning strike twice in the same place?

I couldn't call Allan again. There is a limit to what you can ask of any man and, anyhow, where Allan was concerned, I had no rights. I had made that clear. But I couldn't hold out on the police, either. It was unfair to withhold information that might help them find Mr. Hatfield when, after all, I was depending on them to find Mike.

The commentator's voice rose on a note of excitement. "This information just in. The body of a man beaten to death and concealed behind some garbage cans in a Greenwich

72

Village alley has just been identified as the missing Fillmore Hatfield. Because there were no papers on the body and the fingerprints were not on record and the face had been almost destroyed by a savage beating, no identification was made until an hour ago when a ring worn by the missing man was identified by Mrs. Hatfield as belonging to her husband."

I switched off the set and sat staring at the blank screen. The man who had been murdered in the alley outside my bedroom window was Fillmore Hatfield. The wildest conjectures tumbled over each other in my mind. In the long run I dialed the familiar number of the travel agency and Tommy answered promptly.

"This is Kate. I think I'd better see you."

His tone sharpened. "Anything wrong?"

"That body they found in the alley yesterday afternoon was Fillmore Hatfield. The news is on television. I'll have to tell them—tell the police—he came here."

"Well?"

"What shall I tell them?"

"What do you mean?"

"He came here to see you and he was angry. I can't possibly tell them that."

"Oh." I could picture Tommy's fingers drumming on the desk. "All right, take it easy. I'll be right down."

He came in a couple of minutes, wearing dark slacks and a white turtle-neck sweater. He did not seem to be in the least upset. He was almost casual—carefully casual, I thought. He glanced around. "Was your little brother disjointed at missing all the excitement?"

"Mike! No. He's missing. He disappeared yesterday morning and no one has seen him since."

Some of the studied nonchalance died out of Tommy's face, which warmed with sympathy. "You poor kid! Have you called the police?"

"Oh, yes. That's one reason why—You see, I called them in the morning about your father and then last night about Mike and this morning I went to the Missing Persons Bureau but they didn't take me seriously. They think it's a typical kid's prank and he'll turn up when he feels like it."

"They may be right, you know. Now what did you hear about Fillmore?"

"I don't see how you missed it."

"I haven't been watching television. I've been going over the books and records to find out what the agency's financial situation actually is."

"It's a big story because he was so prominent. It's probably on all the stations."

Tommy found one that was relating the known facts (a few) and giving background material (a lot). Only remaining child of a family that represented four generations of wealth and power. A secret marriage to an actress named Luisa Bara. A cold-blooded killing.

I remembered how ineffectual the man had seemed when he had appeared in the office, not the kind of person to whom dramatic and sordid things happen. But not the kind, either, to marry a glamorous actress. I'd have imagined a plain, sensible girl who was an ardent church-goer and who would share his taste for philanthropy. All I was sure of was that he had been afraid—genuinely afraid. What I tried to prevent myself from acknowledging was that it was Tommy whom he feared. Evidently the hostility between the two men had been real and deep, and Hatfield, not a brave man, had screwed his courage to the sticking point to come to the agency and confront Tommy.

Mr. Hatfield, the commentator said, had last been seen leaving his hotel by the Lexington Avenue exit. His wife knew only that he planned to lunch with her in their suite at one-thirty.

No further information could be obtained from Mr. Hatfield's widow, who was in a state of collapse and, according to her physician, in no condition to be interviewed.

To compensate for a lack of real information, there were hastily gathered stories about Mr. Hatfield's widespread business interests, his clubs, his philanthropies, though the greater part of his work in this field, according to a close associate who chose to be anonymous, was Mr. Hatfield's favorite form of charity, the private benevolence, untold sums provided to help those who, as he had often observed with compassion, were unable to help themselves. According to this unnamed associate, this was the work from which he derived the richest results in personal satisfaction.

"And there," Tommy commented lightly, "we hear the unmistakable accents of Dan Summers."

"Did Summers know Mr. Hatfield?"

"Through and through. None better."

Pictures of the dead man were flashed on the screen; not, of course, as he had been found, but as a timid little boy standing in an impressive room that dwarfed him; one of a row of college boys (third from the left); one in evening clothes, attending a banquet at which he donated a million dollars for the establishment of summer camps to build sound minds in sound bodies. He seemed ill-at-ease and rather shy, but there was a curious look of self-satisfaction around his mouth that surprised me, remembering how it had twitched with nerves when he had talked to me. Perhaps, after all, Fillmore Hatfield III could not be fitted into any simple category. Shy, uncertain, frightened, but with a vein of self-righteousness that could make him easy to dislike.

There were also pictures of his bride, Luisa Bara. These were obviously publicity pictures provided by her agent, and hardly the kind Hatfield would have liked seeing made public. She had knowing eyes under heavy lids and a come-on smile; she didn't look very bright, but very, very knowledgeable. And she seemed oddly familiar, though I could not recall ever having seen her before. So that was the kind of woman who had attracted Hatfield. I supposed, in all honesty, that she would attract most men.

Impatiently Tommy switched off the set. And then there flashed a vivid picture through my mind of him leaning far out of the window on the alley and then drawing back, looking sick.

As usual I blurted out my thought. "You knew who he was yesterday!"

III

It was a long time before Tommy spoke. "Kate, the girl detective," he said almost gently, but his voice made me feel cold. He began to laugh. "Your face! Did you think you were confronting a murderer? Relax, my child. You are—so far—quite safe in my hands." He snarled in a fair imitation of Humphrey Bogart, "But don't get any ideas, sweetheart."

"That's not funny."

"How right you are." He opened his cigarette case, saw

76

that it was empty, and snapped it shut. He began to prowl around the room. Unexpectedly he demanded, "Why did you call me instead of calling the police with this important information?"

"He died practically on your doorstep. And he had come here to see you. He was afraid of you. I couldn't tell the police all that." When he made no comment, I demanded, "Well, could I?"

"Being you, I suppose you couldn't." He skirted the couch where I was sitting and took a straight chair, his head held at its usual jaunty angle, almost as a kind of defiance. "If you think all that looks bad, wait until you hear the rest of it! That's why I've been working so hard, trying to drive it out of my mind. If there were still an electric chair in New York, I'd be headed right toward it. You couldn't ask for a prettier case."

I didn't say anything; there wasn't anything to say. I sat with my hands gripped hard together.

"Okay, I recognized that ring with the scarab on Fillmore's right hand. A conspicuous thing and not characteristic of him. As you must have noticed, he was conservative about his appearance, but he claimed the ring brought him luck. Naturally I didn't recognize—couldn't recognize—" He closed his eyes as though shutting out the picture in his mind. "He'd been beaten until his face was a pulp. No face at all, really; just red meat."

"Don't." I choked, and then as usual, "Sorry; I shouldn't have said that."

"Why not? I had no right throwing a horror like that at you."

"But it's better to get the whole thing out of your system.

77

Then you can forget it."

"I'll never forget it."

"Tommy, have you eaten anything today?"

"No, I couldn't. I wasn't hungry."

I went into the kitchen and reheated the vegetable soup, which, thank goodness, is one thing that improves the longer it stands, scrambled eggs and toasted English muffins and made fresh coffee. It wasn't much, but it was better than nothing. I set a place at the table and called Tommy.

"You eat every scrap of that."

He smiled at me and my heart melted. I'd need all the defenses I could muster against Tommy and I was afraid I didn't have enough. Then I thought of Allan and I felt as though he had created an invisible but invincible shield between me and Tommy's charm—one that would keep me safe.

Until he had finished eating, Tommy did not speak at all. Then he said, "Thanks a lot, Kate. That was just what I needed, but I didn't realize it. You're good for a guy, you know. For this guy, at any rate." I did not return his smile and, suddenly, as though reading my thoughts, he said, "Sorry. I forgot Allan has first claim. Lucky Allan."

I put the dishes in the sink and came back to the living room.

"All right," Tommy said at last, "you want to know why I didn't rush to the aid of the police and identify Fillmore's body at once."

"And save his wife some of the anguish she must have been suffering."

He gave a hoot of laughter. "Luisa's anguish! That's a truly beautiful thought." He came to sit beside me on the

78

couch, but at the far end, hands clasped between his knees, head bowed. "All right, here's the case against Tommy Eakins, and if you can find a flaw in it, that's more than I can do."

"You don't have to tell me anything," I said swiftly.

"Yes, I do. And even if—you know so much already it's better for you to know the whole situation. According to the commentator, Fillmore was killed between ten and eleven in the morning and I entered this house at eleven-thirty. I had lied about being on the ship; I had been right here in New York, living at a hotel under another name, waiting for the ship to dock before I showed up. And I haven't an alibi for the time when he was killed. I was sitting in my hotel room reading *The New York Times*.

"I had flown home for the sole and dishonorable purpose of seeing Luisa Bara. I'd had an affair with her but it was over. *Fini. Kaput.*" He looked at me, looked away again. "I wasn't the only one, and I wasn't the first. Not by a long shot. There had been, are, and will be, a lot of men in Luisa's life. She wasn't important to me in any way. Try to understand that. Anyhow, she wrote me in Athens, saying she was going to marry Fillmore, but she and I could continue having— fun, as she put it, as Fillmore needn't know.

"Well, I've done some fairly rotten things in my life, but not that rotten. It wasn't that I liked Fillmore or that we had been friends for a long time. Actually, I hated his guts. But I don't play that kind of trick and, in Fillmore's case, it would have been unspeakable. Which brings me to the next point.

"Fillmore and I had been—not exactly rivals, but we had competed before for the same girl, for certain awards in

79

college, one thing and another. Somehow, we kept running into each other, and every time I came out top man. Well, you can't do that to Fillmore. He always—" Tommy hesitated. "This sounds melodramatic and yet Fillmore was never melodramatic. The thing is, when he lost, he took his revenge. One way or another.

"In my case, he dropped in to see Dad. I'd been playing around a lot and Fillmore told my father that he had a genuine affection for him. He'd like, in a way, to take my place. Dad," and Tommy grimaced, "said no one could take my place. Fillmore said at least he wanted to be allowed to help. At that time Dad was clerking in a travel agency, making a small salary. Fillmore offered to set him up in his own agency. And he did. He turned over this building to him." Tommy's eyes were hot with anger. "You see it, don't you? There was no real hope of creating a profitable business down here in this out-of-the-way spot. Fillmore did not really want my father to succeed. He simply wanted him to feel grateful and me to feel indebted.

"When I found out about it, I was furious but I couldn't say that I didn't want Dad to have his chance. Fillmore must have laughed himself sick, knowing how I felt and that, for as long as I lived, I'd owe him a debt I couldn't pay. And, of course, I couldn't explain to Dad; he was so tickled over the whole deal, so—grateful." There was an ugly note in Tommy's voice now.

"So we come to the next point. When I got Luisa's note, I knew this was something that had to be settled once and for all. Letters were no good. A telephone call would be no good. So I got Gus, who was second in command of the tour, to cover for me and I flew home, saw her, took her to a night

80

club where we weren't likely to be recognized, and laid it on the line. We were through, permanently.

"You see why I couldn't have told Dad? He would have been outraged at the idea of my treachery to Fillmore though, while I was seeing Luisa, Fillmore wasn't even in the picture. But here I was, hiding in New York, no alibi, using a false name, and waiting for the ship to dock before I could show up. And the hell of it is that I was seen with Luisa at the Boul' Mich'."

"So she was the luscious dame Summers saw you with."

"Got it in one. Of all the damnable luck!"

"But won't he tell the police?"

Tommy laughed. "Won't he! I can't imagine why he's held his hand this long. He hates my guts."

"Why?"

"Because Luisa was his girl when I met her and Dan is—was Fillmore's chief aid and support, his spokesman, his public relations man, his interpreter to the world, his errand boy, his stooge."

"Why did he come here, Tommy?"

"I think he came to laugh in my face. Knowing Dan, that's what he would do."

"But why?"

"Because, though he has held out—so far—on the police, I'd bet my last cent he went straight to Fillmore and told him he'd seen me playing around with Luisa."

"What would he gain by that if he had already lost her?"

"Well, of course, he had a personal score to settle with me, and Fillmore paid handsomely for any little tidbits of information. In fact, I think Fillmore lost no time at all and that it was at his instigation that Dan put that piece in the paper about the bankruptcy. That would be Fillmore all over. He giveth and he taketh away. And that news item was the last thing my father ever saw."

Tommy reached for his cigarette case again, snapped it shut.

"So that's why Summers said if he had made a mistake, he would try to set it right."

"Well, that's the case against Tommy Eakins for the murder of Fillmore Hatfield the Third. You have to admit that it's a beaut. When you call the police and tell them that Fillmore came here, looking for me and breathing fire, that he had already tried to destroy my father's business, and that I arrived on the scene just after he must have been killed, the end will be in sight."

Seven

"I'm not going to tell them," I said at last.

"Why not?" Tommy spoke in a jeering voice that I did not like. "Have you no obligations as a citizen? Surely a fine, upstanding girl like you won't hold out on the police."

I ignored his tone, whose mockery jolted me. It was, I felt sure, a kind of defense mechanism. "Because," I told him, "there's too much against you. Oh, don't laugh! You may be a playboy, but you aren't such a dope that you'd set up a situation like this, kill the man right beside your own building, and hide out for a week when at least one man from that cruise knew you weren't on it. You know what? It sounds to me as though you'd been set up for this murder. There can't be any other reason for Hatfield being killed where he was."

"Well, of course I was set up for it. But what chance do I have of proving it? By the time the prosecution got through outlining the case against me, I'd be halfway to Sing Sing, and if New York still had the electric chair, I'd be all set to fry."

"Stop that!" I said sharply. "You just stop that, Tommy

Eakins. You seem to forget that we don't try people the way they do in Communist countries. It's not all in the hands of the prosecution. There's a defense too."

"What defense?"

"Stop being so defeated. You've got to fight back!"

"Fighting shadows is a singularly unprofitable pastime."

"Oh, go on back to the agency and just give up. Bury your head in the sand. Let someone kick you around! Don't raise a hand in your own defense."

Unexpectedly he began to laugh. He ruffled my hair. "Okay, redhead. Henceforth you may regard me as Tommy the Trojan, charging the barriers. Only just where do you suggest that we start?"

"We?" I said unwisely.

"Well, you can't push me into the ring and not stand in my corner, can you?"

I found myself smiling back at him. No matter how outrageous Tommy was, he had an irresistible quality that I distrusted and yet succumbed to, much to my own irritation.

"All right," I said, "let's start with the obvious question."

"What's that? Who killed Fillmore?"

"No, who hated you enough to set you up as the killer?"

Tommy shook his head admiringly. "No one looking at you would suspect that such deep thoughts were burgeoning behind that pretty face."

"Oh, shut up. This is serious. This is murder, Tommy."

"I haven't forgotten that for a moment," he said soberly. "Well, now," and there was no frivolity in his manner, "the one who really disliked me most was Fillmore himself, but obviously he's out of it. Very much out of it. Then there's Dan Summers who, for some reason I cannot fathom, is not

84

telling the police about my meeting with Luisa or about Fillmore's quick retaliation in putting in the bankruptcy notice."

"Anyone else?"

"If anyone else hates me that much, I don't know who it is and I don't know why. I haven't stepped on any other toes that I know of."

After a thoughtful pause I said, "So far as I can see, the only people who knew you were in New York were Luisa herself, Dan Summers who saw you with her, Mr. Hatfield whom Dan told, and your friend on the cruise ship. Oh, and Allan, of course. But he didn't know until later when I told him about Mr. Hatfield coming to the agency and being afraid and that he'd got the idea you were in New York."

"You really unburden your little heart to Allan Drummond, don't you?"

"Naturally," I said coldly.

"Naturally," he agreed. "Well, Allan's a straight guy. He won't talk unless he really has to. Bless you, Kate, you've given me a shot in the arm. Maybe there is a chance, after all. But what I can't figure out, to save my soul, aside from Dan's ominous silence, is how a man as well-known as Fillmore could be cut down outside this building in broad daylight and not be noticed by anyone for hours and hours. That seems so improbable that I can't understand it at all."

"Well, of course, his body was concealed behind those big garbage cans and no one would have any reason to go down the alley. Someone must have been waiting, just inside the alley, who called as he went by, got his attention, and struck him down when no one was passing. Hardly anyone walks down this street on Saturdays. The people in the apartment building go the other way to do their shopping and take the subway."

"Then the someone who was lying in wait for him must have known that he was coming to the agency. It has to be that way, Kate. But it was taking a hell of a chance. Perhaps there aren't many people on the street, but there are windows. What's wrong?"

"Mike! Our bedroom windows are on the alley. The policeman told me I had a box seat to the whole thing. Mike could have seen anything going on outside his window. If he saw the murder, it would account for his frantic call to Joe. And if he could see out, the murderer could see in. That would —and Mike broke off his call so fast. Oh God, Tommy, if Mike's disappearance has any connection with the murder of a man of Hatfield's importance, he is in terrible danger, isn't he? If he saw the murder, he'll never be released alive."

I clutched at his sleeve and Tommy covered my hand with his own. "Hey, I thought you were a girl who could cope with anything. Now let's take a straight look at this business. Doesn't it seem unlikely to you that if your brother saw anything as terrible as that murder—and that was a vicious murder, Kate—that he would call a kid of his own age and not the police?"

"I don't know. Joe said Mike was terribly upset. Maybe he just wasn't thinking straight. A shock like that—"

"Is this Joe the kind you can rely on?"

"Well, no." The telephone rang and I rushed to answer it.

The voice at the other end was hoarse, blurred. "Miss Forbes? If you want to see your brother alive, do not make any attempt to find him." The connection was broken. I sagged over the telephone and Tommy came to take it out

86

of my clenched hand and put his arms around me. "What is it?" he asked gently.

I repeated the message to him. "So now we know. The kid's been abducted." I tried to stop shaking. "I'll have to call the police."

"After that warning?"

"Kidnapers use the ugliest kind of blackmail. They play on fear of what will happen to someone you love. But every time someone yields to blackmail—"

"The principle is right," Tommy agreed, "quite right. Every time someone surrenders to threats, he opens the way for another victim and another. Oh, I agree wholeheartedly with the principle, but the trouble is that you can't suffer for your own principle, though you are probably willing to go to the stake for it. It's Mike you are condemning to suffer for it."

"But what can I do? He's in danger—awful danger—isn't he?"

"Kate, if Mike did see Fillmore's murder, and we're just guessing about that, and you call the police now, I wouldn't give a red cent for the kid's chances."

I faced him directly then. "How do you know?"

"Look, Kate, try to believe me, if you can."

"Why should I?"

"I don't know why, but please do. I'm telling you the truth. I'll always tell you the truth. If we go to the police about that threatening call, we'll stir up the devil's own cauldron. Leave it to me."

"What can you do?"

Something in my tone made him flush. "You don't think I'm much of a guy, do you? But there's a fellow I knew in the service; he was with the Intelligence. I don't know just what he is doing now, but he can see as far through a brick wall as the next man. He's a good guy, a straight shooter, with a mind like a finely honed knife. He doesn't miss a trick. Will you let me try to interest him?"

"What choice do I have?"

"Look here, my girl, I don't know what you are thinking, but we have to get one thing clear. Do you believe I had anything to do with what happened to Mike?"

"No, because you were right here when the telephone call came."

"So I was. Fortunate, isn't it?" He was angry all the way through, or seemed to be. He dialed a number. "Clark Dixon? This is Tommy Eakins . . . Well, not so hot at the moment. In fact, we have an unholy mess here. Something that, I hope to God, is up your alley. . . . A combination of a murder and a missing person . . . Well, you might say so. The murdered man is Fillmore Hatfield . . . Right away if it is humanly possible. You'd better come here where you can look the thing over *in situ*. It might give you some ideas. I'm fresh out of them. It's the agency address, but come to the basement, will you?"

II

Clark Dixon was a big man, about six foot four, not over-weight, but with a large frame. He had a square face, tanned as though, even after a long winter, he had managed to get some outdoor life. His features were big and blunt, with a wide mouth that turned up sharply at the corners, and a friendly grin. It was, somehow, a good face, not good-looking, but the kind anyone would trust at first sight. The kind of face a successful con man must have. He walked like a cat —light and swift and sure.

Tommy introduced us, explaining that, during his absence, I had been his father's assistant in the agency.

"It was good of you to come, Clark. We appreciate it." Clark grinned. "You sure know how to bait a hook. Fillmore Hatfield no less!"

Tommy turned to me. "It's your story, Kate." He did not ask me to withhold anything. He was leaving it squarely up to me, which was unfair, but he apparently felt sure enough to risk his life or at least his freedom on my discretion.

Clark was easy to talk to. So I told him about Mike and his insatiable curiosity and how he had once tracked down a malefactor whom he noticed stealing one of Allan's ceramics.

"He sounds like quite an enterprising boy."

"He is." I went on to say that Mike had not come home all day Saturday, but I hadn't worried about him until nearly eight o'clock in the evening.

Clark's eyebrows rose. "Eleven years old. Was that usual?"

"No, but it hadn't been a usual day." So I told him about finding Mr. Eakins's body and Clark interrupted with shocked and genuinely concerned surprise. Like everyone who had known Mr. Eakins, he had liked him. He said they had often played chess in the evenings when Tommy was away.

"Of course I knew he had a bad heart. He made no secret of it, but he never made a production of it either."

"Well," I said, when his attention came back to me, "I called the Blanchards with whom Mike had planned to spend

89

the day. They have a son about his age and for his birthday his parents had bought him a German police dog, and Mike had saved his allowance to buy a present. But when I called them, they said Mike wasn't there, he hadn't been there all day. Their son had had a telephone call from him saying something awful had happened and he did not know how to handle it. And then he rang off in a hurry. Or was cut off. And when he didn't come home by eleven, I called the Missing Persons Bureau who seem to think he ran away on purpose. So at three in the morning I called a friend of mine."

Tommy stirred in his chair but he did not speak.

"Then this morning Allan went with me to the police and they more or less politely brushed us off. They seem to think all eleven-year-olds run away at one time or another and it isn't important. And then—just now—I got a telephone call saying if I want to see Mike again, I'm not to try to find him."

"And that," Tommy put in smoothly, "is why Kate is afraid to report to the police. She doesn't want to risk endangering Mike."

"What do you think this is?" Clark asked. "A kidnaping?"

"I think Mike saw Hatfield's murder. It took place in the alley right outside our bedroom windows. And I think either Mike followed the murderer, which would be like him, or the murderer saw him at the window and took him away. And that's why I'm so frightened, Clark." We had got on first-name terms at once. "A kidnaping for ransom does not seem likely, because we have no money. But if Mike actually knows anything about the killing of a man as important as Mr. Hatfield, he must be in terrible danger. In fact, I can't see much hope that he'd ever be released. So then Tommy suggested calling you."

90

This was as much of the story as I cared to tell. The rest belonged to Tommy. I was not going to let him put on my shoulders the responsibility of revealing the extent to which he was involved in the Hatfield murder.

Clark was silent for so long that Tommy began to fidget. At once Clark's attention was called to the drumming fingers and Tommy, becoming aware of it, folded his arms.

Clark said, "This has been a pretty tough time for a little girl like you. Finding Mr. Eakins that way—"

"And the worst of it," I said, "is that we think his heart attack may have been caused by a shock." Too late I was aware that Tommy had become absolutely still, hardly breathing, his face as impassive as he could make it.

"What kind of shock?"

Helplessly, because I was trapped by my own incurable habit of blurting out my thoughts, I told him about the scrap of newsprint I had found clutched in the dead man's hand.

"If I knew your father as well as I thought," Clark said to Tommy, "he would never have taken such a step without consulting you."

"Of course he wouldn't," Tommy agreed. "I've been going over our books and records all morning to see how we stand, but I haven't had enough time. I had to go to the police precinct and then make arrangements and all that."

"Do you have that bankruptcy notice?"

"It's on my desk upstairs. Shall I get it?"

"Later. Now, Kate, as I understand it, you had occasion to go up to Mr. Eakins's apartment. Was that your usual custom?"

"No, actually it was the first time I'd ever been there, or even worked on Saturdays. I always spend Saturday morning

91

shopping with Mike and getting the laundry done and things like that. But Mike was to go to the birthday party and Mr. Eakins was so eager to see his son as soon as the ship docked that I offered to keep the agency open for him. And then I thought he had overslept and I wouldn't have disturbed him, only something came up that I couldn't handle alone."

"What was that?"

"That's where Mr. Hatfield comes in."

Clark stopped in the middle of lighting a cigarette and then shook out his match. "You really have something of the Scheherezade narrative technique."

"He told me he had been married secretly and he was living with his bride under the name of J. Hyde at the Waldorf and, because he wanted to go away on his honeymoon without the media knowing anything about it, he had come to me. That's what I went up to ask Mr. Eakins about.

"Well, Mr. Hatfield left about ten-thirty, but it was nearly four o'clock in the afternoon when there was an uproar in the alley where his body had just been found, except that no one knew who he was then." I ground to a halt, so afraid of my unruly tongue I could hardly speak.

"The point is," Tommy said smoothly, "Kate thinks she is probably the last person, except for the murderer, to have seen Fillmore alive."

Clark spoke to me though his attention never wavered from Tommy. "So you think there's a link between Hatfield's murder and the disappearance of your little brother. Tell me again what the man said over the telephone. It *was* a man?"

"Well," I said, surprised, "I thought so. Just a husky voice that was hard to understand. I suppose a woman with an exceptionally low voice—but no, a woman couldn't handle

Mike, not against his will. He's strong and active for his age. In fact, I can't see how anyone managed to take an intelligent and aggressive boy like Mike away if he was unwilling to go. He'd raise an awful rumpus."

Clark sat relaxed in his chair, his long supple fingers quiet except for the occasional lifting of the cigarette to his lips.

"Tell me about this Joe, where he lives, and how much you can rely on him."

I told him about the Blanchards and their charming house hidden in the garden behind an apartment building next door. Clark nodded. "I've heard of them; they're both well-known and highly regarded in their fields. He's a first-rate sculptor and she produces Off-Broadway shows. Good stuff with a growing subscription audience of the faithful. Some of it eventually gets to Broadway. What about the boy?"

"He's bright enough and Mike believes in him, but I think he's a liar."

"I'll have a talk with him."

"You can't reach him for a few days; the Blanchards have gone out of town because of an illness in the family."

"I'd like to look at the scene of the crime," Clark said. He smiled at me. "It makes me sound so professional." When he stood up, he dwarfed the room. "How about it, Tommy?"

So Tommy took him into Mike's bedroom and I could hear them at the window, though they could have seen nothing outside in the dark. Evidently Tommy was pointing out the spot where Hatfield's body had been found. Then they tramped through the living room and on up to the street and around to the alley, leaving Mike's light burning so Clark could determine how easily he could have been seen from outside.

From my own window I watched them. Clark had a flashlight and he was looking up and down the alley, at the garbage cans, which were now nearer the back door of the restaurant and asking, so far as I could judge by his gestures, how they had been placed at the time of the murder and how Hatfield could have been concealed for so long.

It was a short block and the restaurant took up a good deal of space at the far end. There was a gleam of light and then the back door was flung open and I saw the high white hat of the chef who stood there, shouting. Then his voice dropped and the men talked for a few minutes.

When at last they returned, Tommy looked very queer indeed. Clark sat down in a leisurely way. "You were asking," he said in his gentle voice, "how anyone could get a small boy off the street without the kid making a scene. It seems that a twenty-gallon garbage can was taken from the alley yesterday."

I looked at him blankly.

"Can't you see, Kate, that is how a small boy could disappear from the street without attracting attention. He could have been taken away in a garbage can. It would be plenty big enough to hold a small boy."

"But that's just silly. It would be easier to carry off Mike than to carry a twenty-gallon garbage can with Mike inside. And it would require two people, unless one was as big as you."

"I was thinking in terms of a pickup truck or even the trunk of a car. But I think a pickup truck would be more likely."

"But a pickup truck just happening to be there at the right time—that would mean someone was waiting; someone knew Hatfield was coming to the agency."

"And that," Clark said, "brings me to the big question."

"What did Mike see?"

"No," Clark said in his gentle voice, "the big question is this: Why was Hatfield killed in the alley beside the Eakins building? This job was obviously planned in advance; it was no spur-of-the-moment impulse."

"People are mugged and robbed every day," Tommy pointed out. "The fact that it was Fillmore might be sheer chance; it must have been sheer chance. After all, that's what happened to Kate's parents."

"Muggers don't usually go around in pickup trucks."

"You've postulated a pickup truck but there's no evidence that one ever existed or that Mike was taken away, hidden in a garbage can." Tommy was angry.

Clark sat staring at the polished tip of his shoe for a long, unnerving moment; then he looked at Tommy. "What did you think I could do for you that the police couldn't do?" When Tommy failed to answer, he said, with a touch of impatience, "Look here, Tommy, this story doesn't hold water. It's as full of holes as a sieve. What are you holding back?"

"Believe it or not," Tommy said, "every word Kate and I have told you is the truth." And the ring in his voice should have carried conviction. But, of course, we'd left out a lot.

Clark returned to his absorption in his polished shoe. "Friendship is friendship," he said at last, "but I don't like being used. I don't like being a cat's-paw. And I don't like leading with my chin when I don't know the score. You're ducking the police for some reason of your own, Tommy."

Tommy's fingers drummed on his knees. Then he said, "If

95

Kate goes to the police with her theory about Mike's disappearance and repeats that telephone warning, dragging in the whole thing so that it ties up with Fillmore's murder, what chance do you think the boy will have? The media will grab it and worry it like a dog with a bone. Are you willing to take personal responsibility for that decision, for that boy's life? As I told Kate, it's all right to die for your principles, but it's damned unfair to make someone else die for them."

"You told Kate that, did you?" Clark took out his cigarette package and offered it to Tommy, who refused. "You've quit?"

"In the process. Down to three a day and I've had this day's quota."

"I wondered what made you so nervous. It keeps a guy on edge, doesn't it?" Clark let smoke from his cigarette drift across Tommy's face. It was deliberately provocative. "When did you get back from your cruise?" he asked idly.

Tommy did not look at me. He did not have to. He knew, damn him, that I wouldn't betray him. "The ship docked yesterday morning. This was a big job, over a hundred people. If you've ever a desire to change jobs, you can nursemaid a hundred and two people around the Greek Islands for weeks, look for missing luggage, try to find English-speaking waiters, hire a classics scholar to go along and lecture to people whose natural taste is for the late-late show. It's a dog's life."

Clark stood looking down at me, not smiling. He was not unfriendly, but he had gone out of reach. "Good night, Kate. I hope you find your little brother."

"You aren't going to help?" I wailed.

"Not unless I have something to work with. 'Night,

Tommy. Be seeing you around—I suppose." He was gone so swiftly that I was bewildered.

Tommy looked as though he had been struck in the face. He shook his head as though to clear it. "I'm sorry, Kate. I blew that one, didn't I?"

Eight

That night I did not sleep at all. My worry about Mike intensified by the hour. I went over and over that menacing telephone message. I had read of what happened, over forty years ago, when the more unscrupulous elements of the press learned of the kidnaping of the Lindbergh baby, the men and women who had gathered like jackals outside the home of the agonized parents, the fake telephone calls, the attempt of gangsters and the corrupt or the mentally confused to get in on the act.

Once Mike's disappearance was linked with the Hatfield murder, I'd never see him again. I couldn't take the chance. The man who had administered that terrible beating to Fillmore Hatfield must not be allowed to destroy Mike.

And Clark Dixon, big and reliable and kindly, had refused his help because he believed Tommy was lying or, at least, holding back essential facts. As, of course, he was.

On the other hand, to have admitted that Tommy had been hiding in town all week, that he had had an affair with Hatfield's wife, that Hatfield had come to face him with what he knew, or to warn him that, in retaliation, he would wreck his father's business, and, worst of all, to admit that Hatfield had been afraid of Tommy—the whole story was monstrous. Tommy, too, would not have a chance.

Tommy, it occurred to me, was fast becoming an obsession. Unexpectedly I recalled Allan and remembered those words of Hamlet: "Look here, upon this picture, and on this." Tommy with his rakish manner and the laugh in his eyes and the temperament that even his loving father believed needed a steadying hand. And Allan, calm, serene, always there when needed, always helpful, always undemanding. Allan, who was my best friend—and Mike's.

And then it was Monday morning and Mike had been missing for two days. My mind went up and down its dusty road, wondering what he could have seen, what he had attempted to do on his own, what had stopped him. Mike was not born to be a spectator; he always had to be a part of the action. But where was he now? He had to be alive. He had to. Surely he had been alive when that warning had been given me on the telephone.

I wished bleakly that Clark Dixon had not refused his help. Having him behind you would be like having the support of a whole army. And he had refused because he would not let Tommy make use of him.

I bathed and dressed and made the bed and ate some breakfast, moving sluggishly, my body dull and heavy from lack of sleep. I got ready to go up to the agency and, though I knew it was pointless, I wrote a note for Mike and propped it against the little figure of Mother where he would be bound to see it, asking him to call me AT ONCE.

Just as I was leaving the apartment, the telephone rang. It

was Allan. "Any news?"

"Nothing from Mike, but someone called last night and warned me not to try to find him if I wanted to see him alive."

"Good God!" he exclaimed in concern. "Poor Kate!"

"It's not poor Kate; it's poor Mike."

"What are you going to do?"

"What do you think, Allan?"

"I think you should follow instructions. You can't afford to risk anything happening to Mike. He's—special."

"I know," I said huskily.

"I wish I could see you, but I've got to go over to the Red Bank shop this morning. I have some big orders to fill. I'll call you as soon as I get back to town, and, of course, if anything happens, you can reach me there."

"All right."

"Kate? You told me Hatfield came to the agency on Saturday in a panic. I understand his body was found somewhere in the Village. I've been worrying. It strikes me that you must have been about the last person to see him alive."

"I suppose so."

"What do the police think?"

"I haven't told them."

"You haven't told them that he came to the agency and that he was trying to get out of the country because he had been threatened?" Allan was horrified.

"I didn't dare, Allan! I'm terrified that Mike saw the murder done—the only Saturday when he'd have been in the apartment! I think that's why he's been abducted. I don't dare take that risk."

"I—see. Well, it's a hard decision to make, but I think you

should do it. Don't, of course, make any link with Mike's disappearance. But it's an obstruction of justice not to let the police know that Hatfield came to the agency. Don't you agree? They should be told about those threats on his life."

"I suppose so," I said dully.

"I'll call you tonight. Okay?"

When I let myself into the agency, I was startled to see a man seated at Mr. Eakins's desk. Then he raised his head and I realized that it was Tommy. It was unreasonable to be disturbed by the empty place being filled so quickly. After all, it belonged to Tommy now.

"Good morning, Kate. What news?"

"Nothing." I started to take the cover off my typewriter when he said, "Come in here and let's talk. We have some things to discuss, haven't we?"

When I was seated beside his desk, he reached for his case, which held exactly three cigarettes, contemplated them, and then closed the case. His fingers drummed on the desk. "You didn't tell Clark that I was in New York all last week, or about my connection, my former connection, with Luisa, or that Fillmore came here breathing fire about me. Why?"

"That's your job, not mine. You've got to shoulder your own responsibility, Tommy. I'm not going to do it for you, and that's that. I'm not going to let you set me up as your conscience. It's a lousy job for anyone."

Unexpectedly he grinned at my belligerent tone. "When you get to boiling over, you're a cute little trick." When I ignored this, his smile faded. "Okay, I've made a mess of things—a godawful mess. But it's one thing to try to cover for myself and another to take a chance on your little brother's safety. You have a right to make the decision."

"Why do I?"

Momentarily he was disconcerted and then he smiled with his old challenging cockiness. "You know why." Before I could make any denial, he went on, "Well, it's up to you, Kate. Do I call Clark and make a clean breast of it, or don't I?"

"You're doing it again, Tommy, trying to shove the responsibility for your actions off on me."

"Touché." He looked at me for a moment and then lifted the telephone and dialed a number. "Clark? This is Tommy. . . . Okay, the whole story this time. . . . Thank you." He put down the phone and leaned back in that squeaky chair. "Well, the die is cast. Clark is giving us another chance. He'll be along later in the day, after he has done some checking. He didn't say what."

"On you?"

"He didn't explain." Tommy opened a big account book on his desk to indicate that our conference was over and, a little taken aback, I went to my desk in the front office. I took a few telephone calls, one from the police to ask whether Mike had come home, and several from people who had seen the brief notice of Mr. Eakins's death in the paper and wanted to express their regret. He had rated only a few lines of type, while columns were being devoted to the murder of Fillmore Hatfield.

After a couple of hours, Tommy came out, impersonal and businesslike, to dictate some letters, one of them to a man who was interested in a world cruise. When he had finished the dictation, he flicked the last letter with a fingertip. "We don't often get many requests like this. People wanting to take the big luxury cruises go to the big outfits."

102

He opened the case and took out his first cigarette of the day, lighting it deliberately and inhaling deeply, then he leaned back in his chair, nerves relaxed. "Of course, our agency never really got off the ground. Dad's health had already begun to fail and I was busy conducting tours in Europe and the Far East and Central and South America, even the National parks, when I wasn't playing around with women like Luisa. So now you know the kind of heel I am, Kate, and that is fair warning, in case my good intentions don't last, and they don't often last."

For a moment he smoked, enjoying it in the enhanced, concentrated way of the person for whom it is a vanishing pleasure. "Anyhow, this last tour, one hundred two people, was all the proof I need that the whole idea of competition is a mistake. But where we go from here is what I can't figure out."

"I've been thinking about it a lot, Tommy. If you were to limit yourself to one personally conducted tour at a time, taking a small, select group that you could reach through a few judiciously placed inexpensive ads, and going only when you had a full party, all paid up in advance, it would work. I'm sure it would work. It would be more fun for the tourists because it would be personal. Young couples with just a little money and middle-aged people who want to travel while they can still navigate on their own two feet. Not champagne and caviar and dancing and paid entertainment, but something intimate, with time for bypaths as well as the regular tourist routes." I repeated, "And, of course, prepaid."

He laughed at that.

I was too serious to be distracted by his amusement. "They'd be less of a burden and more fun for everyone and

103

you could go on traveling to your heart's content and get paid for doing it. It would work, Tommy. I know it would."

"My God, I believe it would work."

"And you'd be making a living at it."

"You've really been giving this some thought, haven't you?" Tommy shot me a curious look. "And it would work, all right. But you know what it would mean, don't you? A kind of hand-to-mouth existence from one tour to another."

"What's wrong with that? I've lived that way all my life and so did my parents, and they were happy, especially when my mother pitched in to keep things on an even keel."

"Of course, with someone like you—" Tommy broke off. "Oh, no, I have too much sense to get caught in the same trap a second time. You think a lot of Allan Drummond, don't you?"

"I couldn't begin to tell you how much." I reached out to silence the telephone. "Eakins Travel Agency." I handed the phone to Tommy and saw his face change. "Thank you," he said at last. He pushed back his chair. "They've released Dad's body. I can see him now. I don't know when I'll be back."

"Clark's coming," I reminded him.

He looked at me blankly for a moment. "I'd almost forgotten. For a moment I thought it was possible to build a good future. Any future." He laughed. "Okay, I'll be back. If Clark gets here first, ask him to wait. And tell him," and he looked almost as though I were his enemy, "anything you damned well please."

I found myself dreading Clark's return, but he came in as though nothing had happened, gave me his wide, warm smile, and touched my shoulder lightly.

"He's going to be all right. We're going to fight this thing out together."

"Oh, he'll be right back; he wanted to see his father for the last time." Then, belatedly, I realized Clark had been speaking of Mike.

If he noticed my confusion, and Clark was the noticing kind, he did nothing to embarrass me. "I knew you hadn't heard anything or you would have told me at once." He reached for cigarettes, lighted one, and said, "I suggest that we all have lunch as soon as Tommy gets back."

"I don't think he'll feel much like eating. He was very fond of his father."

"But I will feel like eating and I have a big body to feed." Clark looked up as the hinges creaked and nodded casually to Tommy. He crushed out his cigarette and pushed the ash tray unobtrusively away. This time he wasn't using provocative tactics. The sight of Tommy's drawn face had told him that he had endured about as much as he could take.

The three of us had lunch at a famous old restaurant on Sixth Avenue. Over my protest Clark ordered cocktails and what seemed to me a lavish meal, but I found myself eating heartily. Tommy looked better for every mouthful and, between them, he and Clark managed to keep the conversation impersonal and almost gay.

It was just as we were about to leave, and Clark had

dexterously captured the check, that Tommy's spoon rattled on its saucer and I saw the man across the room who was watching all of us with curious intentness. There was no mistaking that good-looking face, for he was by far the handsomest man in the room and he knew it. It was Dan Summers. He made a mock gesture of salute at Tommy, blew me an impertinent kiss, looking amused when he saw Tommy's ill-concealed annoyance, and scrutinized Clark as though memorizing his face.

Before returning to the agency, I went down to the basement to check, but Mike was not there. In the office I found the two men, relaxed and at ease, discussing, of all things, Cassius Clay and speculating about whether he was finished as a boxer.

But when the three of us were settled, Clark said, "Well, let's tee off. And first I'd like an answer to that question of mine, the one I asked last night. Why was Hatfield killed in the alley beside this building?"

"Okay," Tommy said in a spent voice, "here it is: the truth, the whole truth, and nothing but the truth. I think Fillmore was killed there with the plain and simple purpose of setting me up as his murderer. That's not paranoia; it's the only way I can make sense out of it. It's the simple truth."

"No truth is simple," Clark commented.

"Don't be sententious."

"And who," Clark asked coolly, "would want to set you up as Hatfield's killer?"

Tommy started to speak, broke off, drumming his fingers on the desk.

"May I ask who was the good-looking guy in the restaurant who was so fascinated by you and your pretty companion?"

Tommy shook his head and laughed. "You were always about three jumps ahead of me, Clark. That was Dan Summers, Fillmore's henchman, stooge, and what have you."

"And he doesn't like you at all."

"He doesn't like me at all."

"Any idea why?" Clark added patiently, "Look here, Tommy, I'm willing to go on milking information out of you, though it is like milking a cobra, but it would be a lot easier and save a lot of wear and tear if you could manage to be a little more forthcoming."

"Dan Summers dislikes me for a number of reasons, but the chief one," and Tommy's eyes were hard now, hard and defiant, "is that I cut him out with Luisa Bara."

"That name rings a faint bell."

"As of last week she became Mrs. Fillmore Hatfield. Up to then—" Tommy broke off. "God, what a heel I am!"

"Don't let that bother you," Clark said, and Tommy had to laugh.

"Before the advent of Fillmore—and how in the name of God he ever set eyes on her is beyond me—she was mine and before that Dan's and I don't know who else was on the list. She told me herself she had her first lover at fifteen and I doubt if she has been idle ever since."

Clark gave an exclamation and made ludicrous gestures to indicate a voluptuous figure. "That one?"

"That one. A bit-part actress who suddenly made it big. She has just finished making *The Question Mark,* rated X, which is scheduled for release in a couple of months. And

107

that, of course, accounts for the hasty marriage. She wanted to nail Fillmore down before he found out about it."

"Well, now we know what Summers has against you. But what would he have had against Hatfield that would lead to murder? Apparently he was onto a pretty good thing."

"All I can think—and all I've done is try to think—is he figured that as soon as Luisa was free, he could marry her and get access to Fillmore's millions at the same time. And he had to work fast before the news of the movie broke in the press and Fillmore kicked Luisa out, as he would most certainly have done."

"And at the same time Summers would eliminate you as a potential rival."

"No, I had already eliminated myself," Tommy told him. "And that brings me to the really nasty part of this story." He told Clark how he had flown back to New York to put an end to any idea Luisa might have of a continuance of their affair after her marriage. He'd taken her out and laid it on the line.

"Out of regard for Hatfield?"

"Just call it a faint trace of self-respect. Aside from the fact that I wouldn't deliberately doublecross any man, I couldn't do it to Fillmore. Don't mistake me. I hated his guts." Tommy went on to explain what the multimillionaire had done for his father, buying the building and setting him up in the travel agency.

"That's quite a debt of gratitude to carry," Clark commented, his eyes intent.

"Gratitude! He never meant Dad to succeed, in a run-down building in this part of town. He did it to make me wince. He never liked me, but he was the kind of guy who wanted to have people indebted to him, not just in money, but paying through their self-respect and their independence. There was a lot of submerged cruelty in Fillmore, though he kept it banked down with a shield of good works and philanthropy."

"Perhaps he kept too much banked down. Well, get on with it, Tommy, for God's sake!"

So Tommy told him the whole thing, including Summers's call and Fillmore's visit to the agency where he had come to confront Tommy and from which he had gone to be killed.

After a prolonged silence Tommy laughed. "It's quite a nasty mess, isn't it?"

"A very nasty mess," Clark agreed. "So far as I can make out, you think this is a double-barreled crime; someone not only murdered Hatfield but set you up as the patsy by staging the crime in the alley next to the agency, pointing a finger at you. And you assume that man was Summers, that it was Summers who put through that threatening call to Kate about Mike."

"I suppose so. There's no one else."

"What about Hatfield? Did he have any enemies?"

"I wouldn't say that, but he hadn't many friends."

"But someone threatened him," I pointed out. "That's why he wanted to get out of the country. And, until I convinced him, he thought it was you, Tommy."

"And with all that on his mind he didn't go to the police?" Clark was incredulous. "What kind of game are you two playing on me?"

"He said his wife would hate that," I told him.

"You mean she knew that his life had been threatened?"

"I don't know, of course; but from the way he spoke, I

took it for granted."

"And he came here breathing fire about Tommy," Clark said.

"Handcuffs, anyone?" Tommy said lightly, extending his arms, wrists together.

"Shut up," Clark said, "and let's get this thing clear. Kate, you think the man was really frightened?"

I nodded vigorously.

Clark turned to Tommy. "Did you ever, in any way, threaten the man?"

Tommy raised his hand as though taking an oath. "Never, so help me God!"

Clark appeared to be satisfied. "What about this woman Hatfield married? You knew her. Do you think she could have had any knowledge of who was threatening her husband?"

"Good God, I think Luisa probably engineered the whole thing herself! I can't imagine her putting up long with Fillmore. She wanted to marry him before news of that X-rated movie got out and get rid of him before he could divorce her. What she needed was fast timing. Marry, get out, and then at her leisure pick the next man."

"Presumably Summers."

Tommy hesitated. "Well, he may have thought so; it's the kind of game dear Luisa would play, using it as bait. But Dan was never more than one of a crowd, whatever he may have thought. She might lead him on and promise to marry him if he eliminated Fillmore, but I doubt if she ever meant to marry him. No percentage in that, and Luisa always has her eye on the percentages."

"But if she broke her word, she'd be taking the hell of a

risk, wouldn't she?"

"Why?" Tommy countered. "He couldn't convict her without convicting himself."

"What you're saying is that Hatfield was murdered, if not with his wife's connivance, at least with her blessing."

"That's it. A sex pot if there ever was one, but tough! She'd make the Godfather look like a fairy godmother."

Clark pushed back his chair and stood up and again I was aware of how big he was, towering over Tommy's slender frame. "You've given me a lot to think about."

"Are you going to help us?" Tommy asked, and again I was aware of a little irritation at his lordly use of the royal first-person plural.

Clark's answer was oblique. "I'm certainly going to try to unscramble this mess."

Tommy was aware of the somewhat evasive reply. "But you'll pass on anything you find out?"

Again Clark avoided a direct answer. "Oh, that reminds me," he said so casually that I was alerted, "I thought it might be a good idea to check on when you actually reached this country. You checked in at the Commodore as Travis Evans and checked out again at ten o'clock on Saturday morning, giving you just about time to get here when Hatfield left your office. And you'd had several calls. Could Luisa have informed you of where her husband was going?" He nodded and went out, closing the door behind him.

Tommy lighted his second cigarette for the day.

Nine

I had hardly gone to the basement where, automatically, I called for Mike, when there was a light tap at the door. Clark Dixon stood smiling down at me.

"May I come in?"

"Of course."

"I've been lurking in the alley waiting for you. I wanted to see you alone." He touched me lightly on the shoulder, after giving me a long, searching look. "You won't help Mike by breaking down," he said in the gentle voice that seemed so odd coming from the big, powerful man whom, somehow, one would expect to roar, "and you are closer to breaking down than you know."

"Like my mother, I'm deceptive that way." I tried to speak lightly. "People always thought she was too fragile to take anything, but underneath she had a kind of toughness. I have too."

He smiled then. "It's not a question of fragility but of vulnerability." He sat at ease, relaxed, in my biggest chair. "Let yourself go."

112

I shook my head at that. "I have to hold on tight with both hands or I'll simply fly apart. When I let myself imagine what is happening to Mike, what might already have happened—" I steadied my voice with an effort. "And then there's Tommy in this awful mess. It *is* an awful mess, isn't it, Clark?"

"It's a mess, all right," he agreed heavily. "How long have you known him, Kate?"

"Just since Saturday."

"I've known Tommy for some time. You get to know people fast in combat. You couldn't want a nicer guy to have a drink with or go on the town with. Always brimming over with bright ideas, our Tommy. A very plausible fellow. But he's not much like his father, Kate. He attracts women. I don't suppose he always intends to, it's just something in his makeup. But you have enough to handle right now without coping with Tommy. He's fallen for you in a big way; I recognize the symptoms. I ought to. It's happened often enough."

He was deliberately laying it on the line. "Don't mistake me, little Kate. I like Tommy. No one could help liking him—men as well as women. But even in ordinary circumstances I'd dislike having a sister of mine involved with him emotionally because, in the long run, she'd be bound to get hurt. And these aren't ordinary circumstances. There's too much against him right now. A whale of a lot too much."

"So that's when people ought to turn against him."

"That was a tactical error, wasn't it? You're one of those gals why fly to the assistance of the guy who is down. Look here, haven't you any real friends you could turn to at this

113

time? That's what I've been waiting to ask you. Frankly, I'm worried."

"You needn't be. I'm not one bit interested in Tommy." Which was a mistake, of course; any normal girl would be interested in Tommy. "And anyhow, there's Allan Drummond. Allan is always there when he is needed."

"Tell me about Allan."

"I can't honestly see that this is any business of yours," I flared.

Clark grinned at me. "You're like a small chick with all its soft little feathers ruffled up. Go on," he added cajolingly, "tell me about Allan. I suppose he is too kind and trustworthy and undemanding to be interesting. There's no challenge about a man like that."

As this was perilously close to the truth, I was thrown off balance, but I managed to describe Allan, explain how he had come into our lives three years before, the self-styled Friend of the Family, a phrase that made Clark shake his head in commiseration.

"Poor devil, how can he fight an image like that? The faithful confidant who has to listen to a girl's woes over her mistaken love."

I laughed at that. "He's not stuffy, not a scrap." I showed him the ceramic figure of Mother and explained that Allan had designed and made it for her last birthday. Clark turned the figure over and over in his big hand. "This guy has talent. Real talent. And he knows how to use his eyes and translate what he sees into an enduring form of beauty. You could do a lot worse, Kate."

"Don't think I haven't learned to appreciate Allan. He came to the rescue when my parents were killed, settled

114

things, helped us move, sold Dad's business and our little house. He even found me this job. He'd known Tommy from college days."

"And yet he sent you here? Now that's one thing that really surprises me."

"Well," I said, with my ineffable ability to say the first thing that popped into my head, "Tommy was away at the time, of course." And then I could have kicked myself.

"So he wan't trying to throw you to the wolves," Clark commented. "I can think of better ways of protecting you than letting you work here."

"If you mean—does Allan want to marry me, yes, he does. He keeps on asking me but he doesn't push it, partly because he felt he was taking advantage of my being at kind of loose ends and partly because he was just getting started and he doesn't feel he has much to offer."

"Would that weigh with you?"

"Of course not! And the best part is that he is genuinely fond of Mike and Mike is crazy about him and wants to be just like him. He'd take good care of Mike and not think him a burden."

"That's the best part, is it?" Clark looked at his watch and stood up, making the room shrink. "Friends like your Allan are hard to come by. Don't discourage him, honey. It sounds to me as though you and Mike could do a lot worse."

"If Mike comes back."

"Why, of course he is going to come back," Clark said in a shocked tone.

Legs passed the window and someone ran down the steps. Allan came in carrying a big bunch of jonquils, crisp and fragrant and heralding the spring. He thrust them into my

115

hands and looked up in surprise at Clark.

"Clark," I said, "this is my old friend Allan Drummond. Clark Dixon, Allan."

The two men shook hands, summing each other up openly, and, to my relief, mutually liking what they saw. Allan noticed the ceramic figure Clark was holding and looked a question at me.

"It might be Kate," Clark said.

"Kate is a lot like her mother and in more than looks. A little more serious, perhaps, but maybe gaiety will come out later when she hasn't so many responsibilities to clip her wings." Allan picked up the ceramic figure Clark had set on the table. "What a marriage that was! Two people still deeply in love, who complemented each other so completely that they were like two halves that made up the whole. It was a perfect thing, wasn't it, Kate?"

I nodded, not speaking. It came to me with a shock of pain and shame that for two days I had barely thought of the parents whom I had loved. I must be some kind of egotistical monster.

"I take it there's no news," Allan said.

"Nothing."

Allan turned to Clark. Obviously he wanted to know why he was in the basement apartment and where he had come from, as I had never mentioned him before. "Do you know about Mike?"

There was amused understanding on Clark's face. "That's why I am here. Tommy Eakins gave me a call." He could not fail to see the chill in Allan's eyes. "We met during the war in a Saigon bar when it was my unsavory job to smoke out

116

subversives and various skulduggery of that ilk."

"Military Intelligence?"

"Nothing dramatic, you know; just undercover snooping. But apparently I have a flair for the work and when I was discharged, I was offered a job doing some private sleuthing. Sordid, for the most part, but a challenge." Clark rubbed his forehead. "And we can be as fastidious as we like, but after all someone has to do the dirty work. I don't really know why it should be me."

"You mean," and Allan's face was hard with anger, "that Tommy called you in after the warning Kate got?"

I held my breath, but I should have known Clark better by now. "I won't interfere with the police, you know, and apparently they aren't taking much interest in Mike. I'll just poke around privately, seeing what, if anything, I can pick up on my own. I won't take any risk of endangering the boy, Mr. Drummond."

"That makes me feel easier," Allan admitted.

Clark waved a big hand at me. "I'll keep in touch. Don't worry. Let this guy do some of it for you," and he gave Allan his friendly grin. "Looks to me as though he could handle it without any trouble."

When the long legs had gone striding briskly past the window, Allan said, "That's a nice guy, Kate. What do you know about him?"

"Nothing except what Tommy told me, that he can see through a brick wall better than most. I think he's nice and trustworthy, don't you?"

Allan nodded. "Find out what outfit he's with, if you can, without making it too obvious. I'll check up on him, but my

117

guess is that he's a good guy to have on your side. But just the same, I hope you haven't made a mistake in ignoring that warning, Kate."

Seeing that he had disturbed me, Allan switched the conversation away from Clark and while I got dinner he propped his shoulder against the kitchen wall and talked easily. At first I thought he was probing too closely about affairs at the agency now that Tommy was in charge so, to reassure him, I said that Tommy was busy settling his father's affairs and making arrangements for the services, so I saw little of him except when he was dictating. This wasn't the whole truth, of course, but Allan was so disturbed I wanted to reassure him. I didn't succeed.

"I've always warned you that Tommy is not the kind of guy I like seeing around you. It's not just his temper—that vicious, flaming temper of his—because he isn't apt to show that to you. But he's a confirmed chaser. Chasing girls is practically his profession."

"Considering the number of calls I've taken for him," I said, "it's my guess that they chase him."

"Well, if he begins to bother you—"

I laughed and began to talk about Allan's business. Things were beginning to break, he said. Some articles had appeared, one in a trade journal, one in an art magazine, describing his work, showing illustrations, and there was a big feature piece scheduled for the following Sunday Magazine section.

"And that," Allan said, "means that really sizable orders will be coming in. When a thing like that starts, the snowball just keeps getting bigger and bigger. We may not have it made, but we're on the way."

His first-person plural reminded me of Tommy's, but I

118

didn't say so. For the first time since I had known him, Allan seemed to be really happy, almost expansive.

"Of course," he went back to his expanding prospects while we were eating, "I'll have to put out money for a bigger kiln; and, if sales justify it, I can move down from that top floor display room on Madison Avenue to a spot on the street level where I can have a window display. Give me time, girl, and I'll be making Steuben's look like Woolworth's."

"Counting your chickens," I teased him.

"Maybe. But it doesn't hurt to look ahead. In fact," and he reached into his coat pocket, "I have been looking ahead." He pulled out a ring box and pushed it toward me, his eyes intent.

I gave him a startled look, met his smiling one, and opened the box. The ring was set with a very small diamond, but its purpose was unmistakable.

"Allan?"

"Don't say no. You can't say no, Kate. It's not very big, but by this time next year you can have whatever you want." He pushed back his chair and came to me, took the ring out of the box and slipped it on my finger. Then, for the first time in all the months I had known him, he kissed me, not at all the kind of kiss one would expect from A Friend of the Family. Not at all.

"We'll work things out together," he said.

Somehow I could feel Clark beaming approval. "Together," I echoed, but with a feeling that I was sealing my fate, that events were moving too fast for me. Then I rested my head against his shoulder and was aware only of the comfort it gave me.

Allan had not been gone more than an hour, and I was just

119

dropping to sleep, when the telephone rang. At that time of night news is apt to be bad news and my heart pounded so I could hardly hear the voice at the other end of the line. It was Allan.

"Darling," he said, "wonderful news. I've just had a message from Mike!"

"Mike! Is he all right? What happened to him? Where is he?"

"He called from somewhere near Rochester."

"Rochester! Rochester, New York?"

"Of course."

"But what on earth is he doing there? How did he get there?"

Allan laughed. "He hitched a ride on a pickup truck, just for kicks apparently. He said he hadn't expected to go so far. He was a bit sheepish about that."

"But I've warned him and warned him about riding with people he didn't know. I can't believe he'd do it."

"Well," Allan said reasonably, "apparently he has done it. So we know he is safe and sound and well. It's good news, Kate. Really good news."

"But what is he going to do?"

"He said the driver has to make another trip to New York in a couple of days and he'll bring him along. There's one thing sure. He's having a whale of a time. Now I'm going to call the police and you can call off your private bloodhound. We're in the clear. Good night, my darling. Sleep well."

And with the immense relief of knowing that Mike was safe and well, I did.

120

On Tuesday morning, television, radio, and newspapers were still giving major attention to the murder of Fillmore Hatfield, though it was obvious that they had not got much farther toward solving the crime. His multiple business interests were being probed, his friends and associates were being checked, without result. More and more the police appeared to be coming to the conclusion that the murder had been the result of another mugging or, to account for the brutal destruction of the man's face, that it was the work of one of the so-called liberation armies, springing up around the world, inspired by malcontents, the semiliterate, the dope addicts, and the failures who believe they can acquire their proper place in the world only by eliminating the competition.

There was a television interview with Dan Summers, handsome and grave, speaking with the sincerity and enthusiasm of a clothing salesman, telling with tears in his eyes of Fillmore Hatfield, the shy and modest man, his generosity, his private charities, his warm capacity for friendship. A man without enemies. It seemed a final bitter irony that a man of friendship should die brutally and meaninglessly.

According to the media, Mrs. Hatfield, the grieving widow, was still unable to see anyone. She had decided to remain in seclusion at her suite in a midtown hotel, where she would be assured more privacy than in the Hatfield apartment on Park Avenue, with its large staff of servants, some of whom might be open to bribery. Hardly a tactful comment or one likely to inspire loyalty.

"All I ask," Mrs. Hatfield is reported as having said in the one telephone interview she had granted—no calls were now being put through to her suite—"is that the public respect my grief and give me time to recover. Great sorrow following on great happiness is unbearably painful. Please let me have the seclusion and the privacy I need so desperately."

If it was really privacy she was seeking, she was in for a shock if she looked at the paper that morning. Her theatrical agent, presumably without consulting her, had taken advantage of the immense amount of publicity given to Hatfield's death to direct some of it to the grieving widow's forthcoming film, *The Question Mark,* to be released in May. According to her agent, this X-rated picture was to provide a new dimension in the growing need for the honest portrayal of sex in films. Luisa Bara's performance was a bold attempt to break away from the last chains of Victorian prudery. I blinked. Anyone conscious of Victorian chains of prudery must be living in a world of his own.

I put down the newspaper and tried to face my own personal dilemma. Now that I was assured that Mike's disappearance had nothing to do with the death of the multimillionaire, I knew I should go to the police and tell them of Hatfield's visit to the agency, his fear for his life, and his desperate desire to get out of the country as soon as possible, but I was afraid on Tommy's account.

Whether or not Tommy was right about Luisa's complicity in her husband's murder, it seemed more than likely that she had known where he was going that morning. Then why had she held her tongue? Fear for herself? Fear for Tommy who, as she well knew, was in New York?

Again that morning, among the calls about agency business, and the inevitable calls from women wanting to talk to

Tommy, who had not yet put in an appearance, there was one from Clark. "Just reporting so you can see what an active guy I am," he said cheerfully. "You can answer as carefully as you like."

"It's all right; there's no one here. And, Clark, I was just waiting for Tommy to come down to ask for your telephone number." I told him about Mike's call to Allan the night before.

"So apparently the little demon is enjoying himself hugely and he'll be back in a couple of days. And we don't have to worry about him any more, though at this moment I'm in a mood to dismember him and throw the pieces to the wolves."

"Well, I'll be damned! Rochester! Seeing a bit of the world on his own. I remember trying to smuggle myself on board a ship when I was about that age and I got the tanning of my life. Well, that's good news, Kate. When did your friend Allan call?"

"About eleven. And he said I could tell you about it so as not to waste more of your time. He liked you a lot, Clark."

"It's a pity you can't see me smirking," he said, and I laughed. Then he added thoughtfully, "Then how are we to account for that threatening call?"

"I've got a darned good idea that Joe Blanchard thought that one up. It would be just like him. He probably made himself believe it was true. He lives in some grim fantasy world of his own. And I'd like to wring his neck."

"Feeling bloodthirsty this morning, aren't you, in spite of all the good news."

"I guess it's just the reaction."

"What gets me—" he began and stopped.

"What's that?"

"Oh, nothing," he said vaguely. "I'll keep in touch. And if you want to reach me at any time, the number is—got a pencil handy?—" I wrote it down.

"Clark, there's something wrong, isn't there?"

"My dear, I don't have second sight."

"Please don't be evasive. What is it?"

"How could Drummond be sure that it was really Mike speaking to him?"

I caught my breath and then expelled it in relief. "Oh, Allan knows him so well he couldn't be mistaken."

"But does he know him well enough to be sure that he was —well, shall we say talking of his own free will?"

"Clark!"

"Sorry, Kate. Probably there's nothing in it. But we have to look at all sides, you know."

I was still staring at the silent phone when Biddy Blanchard called from somewhere in Connecticut.

"What's the news about Mike?"

I told her about my terror that his disappearance had been linked with the murder of Hatfield in the alley outside our windows, about the menacing call—I didn't mention Joe— and the message Allan had received the night before, saying that Mike was in Rochester, where he had hitched a ride on a pickup truck, that he'd be back in a couple of days, and that he was having a fine time. And, to bring the wheel full circle, Clark's disturbing question about whether Mike was making the call under duress to prevent any further attempt to find him.

"You've really been in hell, haven't you, Kate?"

"It's the waiting. The not knowing."

Being Biddy, she offered no pointless words of sympathy.

124

"I thought I understood Mike and I envied you that—that stability he has. Joe is so sort of fluid you can't seem to get hold of him. But somehow I wouldn't have thought Mike would go off like that, just for the fun of it. He'd know how you would worry."

"According to what he told Allan, he didn't expect to go so far."

"But how many miles is it? The driver would have had to stop for gas. Why, it must be almost a full day's ride. He had plenty of chances to call you unless—" She broke off, appalled by the implications of her own words.

"I know. Unless he couldn't call or did it only under pressure," I said steadily. "That's what Clark suspects; at least it's a possibility."

There was a long silence at the other end of the line and then Biddy said, "In spite of his age, Mike has the best head on his shoulders we've ever encountered and he's good for Joe. I only wish Joe weren't such a dreamy, impractical kid, living in an imaginary world of his own. I suppose," she added gloomily, "he'll turn out to be a writer."

I couldn't help laughing. "A fate worse than death."

"You know what I mean. He lives too much inside himself. Oh, well, of course people have to follow their own drummer."

"Biddy, could Joe possibly have made that threatening call to me?"

"Oh, no!" she exclaimed in horror. Then, more slowly, "Honest to God, I don't know, Kate, but I'll find out. So what do you do now?"

"Wait," I told her. "What else can I do?"

"Nothing, I suppose. I wish to heaven we could be with

125

you, but we'll have to stay on here at least one more day."

"I hope your aunt isn't seriously ill," I said, but without interest. After all, I'd never seen the woman.

"She's never ill," Biddy said in exasperation. "She just gets bored and develops some symptoms to make herself interesting, and she has hysterics if we don't come to hold her hand. We'll be back soon, darling. And I'll take Joe apart to see what makes him tick. Keep your chin up. We love you." Just as I thought she was going to hang up, she said, "You know, I hadn't realized the Hatfield murder took place practically next door. I was so stunned at learning he had married Luisa Bara, I guess I was too shook to notice anything else."

"Had you heard of her?"

"For my sins, and if you quote me I'll do something drastic to you. I wouldn't put it past Luisa to have had a hand in this murder. When I read of the marriage, I nearly fainted. Luisa of all people to marry a pillar of the church. Luisa!"

"Where did you come across her? She doesn't sound like your type."

"You can say that again. She came around a couple of years ago, trying to get a role in a play we were casting. At the time she was down on her luck. She had been doing some singing in a cheap night spot and, when she was really desperate, she became a topless waitress in some Hollywood dump. She told me that Equity had a down on her and she couldn't get a decent part. But she's such a liar I don't know what the truth was. Anyhow, we turned her down.

"She was Louise Bates from Hoboken and she can't act. She has only one talent, so far as I know, and she has exploited that as far as she can go. Next time I heard of her, she was back in Hollywood, linked up with a new outfit, and

126

being cast for the lead in *The Question Mark,* which has been floating around for years without any takers. And good reason. Anyone putting on that thing is risking a stiff jail sentence. And that, by the way, is a nice thought. A very nice thought. Good-by, Sweetie. See you."

Ten

Tommy came down very late, looking as though he had not slept at all.

"Any news?"

I told him about the call Mike had made to Allan, saying he had hitched a ride to Rochester and would be brought back in a couple of days.

His face lighted up. "I'm so glad for you, Kate."

Then I told him about Clark's call and the question it had raised. Had Mike spoken of his own free will or had he been coerced? So I was back on tenterhooks.

Tommy's hand covered mine, closed over it. He felt the ring, looked at it. "Allan's?"

"Allan's."

"He's a lucky guy, Kate. I wish you every happiness. I'll probably be out the rest of the day."

"Wait, Tommy, there are a lot of telephone calls." I put them in his hand and he riffled through them. "I'm still out," he said, crumpling and dropping them into the wastebasket. "I don't know when I'll be back. Maybe never."

When he had gone, I sat turning Allan's ring around and around on my finger. At that moment I needed him more than I had ever needed him in my life. Instinctively I reached for the telephone and then I remembered that he had said he was going to his Red Bank shop and that he would be feverishly busy all day, packing orders and shipping them.

The hinges squeaked, the door opened, and a woman came in—a tall woman with blond hair pulled back so tightly that she reminded me of the Hitler maidens of a past generation. She wore amber glasses and no makeup on a dead-white face. Her black coat was shabby and looked as though it had been made for a much larger woman, hanging shapelessly around her and halfway down her calves. She wore black stockings and flat shoes and carried a cheap black plastic handbag.

She stood looking down at me for a moment without speaking.

"May I help you?"

"I'd like to see Mr. Eakins, please."

"The senior Mr. Eakins died several days ago and Tom—his son is out attending to funeral arrangements."

"When will he be back?"

"He didn't expect to return to the office today."

She lighted a cigarette and tossed the match on the floor. "Who are you?"

"Mr. Eakins's assistant."

"How long have you been working here?" She sounded like a policeman grilling a suspected drunken driver.

"About a month."

"Who are you?"

"The assistant," I repeated, doing a slow burn.

"Haven't you got a name, Assistant?"

"Katherine Forbes. Shall I take a message?"

"You shall take a message. Tell Tommy that Mrs. Stevenson called." She laughed. "He'll know."

Her laughter was echoed from the doorway. Dan Summers came in, looked from me to the tall blond zombie and laughed again. "Well, well. Fancy meeting you here, Mrs. Stevenson. I couldn't be less surprised."

For a moment they weighed each other, the man mocking, the woman furious. "Don't forget the message," she told me, and started out.

Summers reached the door ahead of her and opened it with exaggerated gallantry. "How did you manage it? Freight elevator? You know the temptation to make just one telephone call is almost more than I can resist."

Again that long look. "It wouldn't be worth your while," she said.

"Sure of that?"

"Quite sure. You could do a lot better, you know."

"Okay. I'll take your word, and that doesn't happen to you every day."

The woman's hand clenched convulsively and then she seemed to remember that I was there and that I was listening to every word. "Are you coming my way?" she asked, and I knew she did not want to leave Summers with me.

He knew it too. His handsome face was alight with malicious laughter. "Nothing I'd like better. Another time. But soon. Naturally."

"Naturally. Be careful about getting too much red in your palette, Dan." And then the outer door closed behind her and I heard her walk down the steps to the street.

Summers settled himself beside my desk and, because he

was the noticing kind, he saw the engagement ring at once. "Tommy's?" he asked sharply.

"A man named Allan Drummond."

"Well, well, good old Drummond. To coin a phrase, it's a small world. He's another protégé of Hatfield's, or didn't you know?"

"Yes, Allan has a picture taken with Mr. Hatfield on a Hawaiian vacation years ago, when they were in college together."

"Hatfield recently set him up in business. Took pity on the guy, who was scraping along on nothing, and set him up with a display room on Madison Avenue, with a salesman to take over when Drummond is working at Red Bank, or wherever that jerk place in New Jersey is. Recently I've even arranged for him to get some nice publicity."

Allan hadn't told me that he owed his good luck to Fillmore Hatfield, probably because he did not want me to know that it was an old friend and not an unknown admirer who had backed his project. I recalled how sharply he had rejected the idea of appealing to him for a job for me. Apparently, as with the Eakins Travel Agency, the act of apparent generosity had carried a sting in its tail.

Summers settled himself more comfortably. "Yes, Hatfield did a lot of that sort of thing, small private charities, and it looks to me as though his wife would probably carry on in the same way. Just peanuts, of course, but how Hatfield enjoyed doing them! Got more of a kick out of them in a way than out of a lot of bigger operations." It seemed to me that there was more bitterness than admiration in his tone and I wondered whether Summers, too, might not have been a victim of Fillmore Hatfield's little charities.

He reached over to take my hand and examine the ring more closely. "So Allan got you first. It's not like Tommy to miss out on a good thing. Tommy down yet?"

"He's gone out."

"When do you expect him?"

"He didn't say."

"You aren't very helpful, are you?"

I jerked my hand away. "Why should I be?" Again I was aware of how extremely good-looking the man was and of how much I disliked his handsome face. Obviously my reaction surprised him. Probably not many women resisted his brand of attraction.

"I don't know what you're up to, kid, unless you are playing hard to get, and that's not a good line to take with Tommy. Just a friendly tip." He lighted a cigarette which he took from a gold case and used a gold lighter, giving me plenty of opportunity to admire them both by setting them on the desk in front of me. "Shall we get down to cases? Tommy Eakins is in a bad spot. It could not be worse. He's played around once too often and this time he's got burned. Plenty. I trust the evidence of my own eyes, not what I'm told by a cute little trick like you. Tommy was having an affair with Luisa Bara. When he heard that she was going to marry Hatfield, he flew back to New York to try to prevent it. Don't tell me he wasn't in town. Alibis can be arranged, and I'm the man to break them. Or, if necessary, to break Tommy. I saw him with Luisa at the Village hot spot and told Hatfield. He was my employer and I owed him that."

"That's the kind of thing I'd expect you to do," I said, and sat turning Allan's ring around and around, like a talisman, which, in a sense, it was.

"Let's keep it polite, shall we?" Summers said with that flashing smile. "Even from pretty little redheads I take just so much. And we're about at that point, aren't we?"

"What do you want of me, Mr. Summers? Please tell me and then get out."

"My, my. Well, here it is, short and sweet. Tommy, with or without Luisa's help, and now I'm forced to say with, decided to eliminate Hatfield, get his girl and his money. Now my blinders are off, I'm willing to let him have the girl. At a price. My price."

He took my arm and his grip tightened when I tried to free myself. "Tommy is in a hole, my dear. A nasty hole. I want him to get in touch with me *at once*. No more fooling around." His grip tightened again, hurting me. Next morning I found purple marks on my arm from his fingers.

Then he released my arm and drew me up from my chair in one quick jerk, pulling me against him. He kissed me—ugly, searching, insulting kisses until my mouth felt bruised. When he released me, he was laughing.

"That red hair is for real! It's a pity I haven't more time today. Now here's one thing more to bear in mind. Find out for me where Tommy was staying last week and you'll get a nice bonus. Very nice. Something to help you start married life on." He laughed again and went out of the office, pausing in the doorway to say, "Tell Tommy that time's a-wasting."

II

I'd eaten my sandwich and drunk coffee from the thermos I'd brought up from the basement. For the first time I did not bother to check the apartment. I knew Mike would not

133

be there. Now that Clark had shaken my faith in Mike's telephone message, I wished that Allan had not been so prompt in calling off the police search, if they had ever troubled to make one.

The mailman came in to drop letters in the slots and I decided that I could not endure that creaking one more minute. I took the oil can I had bought a week before and went out into the hall to oil the lower hinges. Then I hauled out a chair, perched on it precariously, and began to work on the upper ones. The door was flung back, hurling me off the chair and onto the floor and the chair fell on top of me.

Tommy pulled it off, picked me up and brushed me off. "Did I hurt you?"

"I'll live."

He climbed on the chair to do the oiling himself, and then took the letters from the boxes and came in, flipping them over. As he started on toward his own office, I said, "Wait, Tommy."

He turned back. "Yes?" His manner was not encouraging.

"Two people came to see you. They both said it was urgent for you to get in touch with them at once."

"Well?"

"She was a Mrs. Stevenson. She wants you to get in touch with her right away."

"Stevenson?" he repeated blankly.

"She laughed and said you'd know."

"Stevenson?" He shook his head. "What did she look like?"

"A blonde with her hair pulled back tightly like a Hitler maiden. Dead-white face like a zombie. Shabby black coat hanging well below her knees, black hose and flat shoes."

When he still looked blank, I added, "Summers came in while she was here. They knew each other. She was overbearing and rude to me and impertinent and wanted to know who I was and how long I'd been here. And I guess she thought the Summers man was interested in me, because she did not want to leave him here. She said something about it wasn't good for him to have too much red in his palette."

Tommy was standing still now, deep lines in his forehead. "Did you hear any more of this interesting conversation?"

I tried to remember. "He said he wasn't surprised to see her here but he wondered how she had managed it or if she'd taken a freight elevator and he was tempted to make just one telephone call and she said he could do better."

Tommy's face darkened. "Stevenson! Oh, what a fool that woman is! I'll bet she never even heard of *Dr. Jekyll and Mr. Hyde* unless Fillmore told her. I doubt if Luisa can read."

"Oh!" When I'd caught my breath, I said, "You mean that zombie was Mrs. Hatfield? But it couldn't have been. Her pictures are so glamorous and not at all like that."

"She came here? Right to the agency? God, what kind of game is she playing?"

"She wanted you to call her at once. Tommy—"

"Don't worry. I have no intention of calling Luisa."

"I wasn't worrying," I said much too emphatically, and I saw the change in his expression. Where women were concerned, Tommy was as quick as a flash. "At least I was worrying, but not about her. About Summers. He came here to say he knows you were in New York last week and he intends to break your alibi and break you, if necessary. And he offered me a bonus to find out where you'd been staying. He believes you killed Hatfield and he says you can have the

135

girl but he wants his own price."

Tommy made a rude sound, but he sobered when I said, "He means it, Tommy. He did see you in New York and the fact that she came here today, disguised as she was, made him positive that you were in this murder together. He intends to make trouble for you. He's—not a very nice man, Tommy."

Tommy gave a half-laugh at that and then he dropped into the chair beside my desk. "How did you cut your lip?" he asked idly. "When I knocked you over?"

"Cut it?"

He leaned forward and touched it gently with a clean handkerchief and showed me the drop of blood.

"Oh, that was Summers," I said before I thought.

There was an ugly flush on his face. "You mean that rat bothered you?"

"He won't do it again. He was just amusing himself." I tried to speak lightly because of the flare of rage in Tommy's eyes. This must be the dangerous temper Allan had warned me about. "Don't look like that, Tommy. It doesn't really matter."

"It matters all right. You don't have to take anything from anyone. I'll have a word with Dan."

"Be careful!"

"He really scared you, didn't he?"

"Yes, he did, but not on my account. Even before he found Mrs. Hatfield here, he was pretty sure you were involved in the killing, and now he's convinced."

"He's trying a double play, Kate. He's the only human being who could have pulled off that murder."

"Well, anyhow, he's out of a job now and he intends to get

136

money somewhere—from you or Mrs. Hatfield or both of you. She was practically promising to meet his demand while they were here. I can understand that now. And I don't think he'd stop at much."

"Neither do I," Tommy admitted. "But, damn it, Kate, the fact remains that I didn't kill Fillmore. I don't know who did, if it wasn't Dan Summers. I still—Look at it this way. Luisa triggered the killing, Dan carried it out. Then he finds that—oh, hell!—Luisa prefers me. He is trying to get his percentage so that even if Luisa marries me—and she won't —he'll be sure of his cut."

"Tommy, why don't you call Clark and tell him about Summers and Luisa and the way things look now?"

"I hate like hell having my hand forced. I'm going to call Summers's bluff."

"But Clark could—"

"He made quite an impression on you, didn't he? What are you trying to do? Mastermind the situation? Take me over, lock, stock, and barrel?"

"I wouldn't have you as a gift," I flared. "But Summers scares me—scares me to death. If you're right about him, then he must be the man who has Mike and who made that threatening call and then changed his tactics and forced Mike to call and say he was all right."

After a long pause Tommy said, sounding tired and spent, "Okay, I'll call Clark. But, Kate, I don't want you involved any more. You'd better get out of here now and marry Allan. At least he has no connection with the Hatfield murder."

"No, of course not, but he does have a connection with Hatfield. The Summers man told me so. Hatfield is the one who set Allan up with his New York display room. And

137

Allan doesn't like him."

Tommy laughed. "Dear old Fillmore. Never at a loss. He latched onto Allan and me in college and three more different people you'd never find. I was winning out with the girls and sports and Allan was winning out in the only other field in which Fillmore wanted to compete—in scholarship. He just had to be top man. He had to make us feel that we were inferior, dependent on him. Damn his soul! If you expect me to express any grief over Fillmore's death—"

"Well, at least I expect you to have brains enough not to go around shouting how much you hated the man! Are you trying to put a noose around your own neck?"

"Termagant!" Tommy brushed his fingertips across my cheek. "I may be careless with my own neck, but I'm not careless about yours—or Mike's. I'm going to call Clark now. Get me an outside wire, will you?" He went into his office and closed the door.

Eleven

Wednesday morning. Mike had been missing for five days. I was just finishing breakfast when the telephone rang. It was Tommy, sounding sober and subdued.

"Kate, this is a lot to ask, but will you go to the services with me?" As I was silent, taken by surprise, he added, "I think Dad would have liked to have you there."

"Of course."

"I'll call for you at eleven, if that's all right, and leave a sign on the door saying that the agency is closed."

"Have you had any breakfast?"

"Coffee. I couldn't eat anything this morning."

I changed to my only black dress, a plain wool with no ornaments, and I went around the corner to buy jonquils and daffodils to have delivered to the funeral parlor. They weren't funeral flowers, which is why I chose them. It was sunlight and not gloom that Mr. Eakins had loved, and they were for him.

It was a sober Tommy who called for me, a black armband sewed awkwardly on his sleeve so that the threads were already loosening. I fixed it properly and we went out to get a cab.

Tommy was sunk in thought and I did not attempt to speak to him. When we reached the funeral parlor, I was surprised to find a dozen or more people sitting quietly in the room with its closed coffin on which my spring flowers glowed, filling the air with their light, fresh scent.

All during the mercifully brief service Tommy sat looking straight ahead of him, while an organ throbbed somewhere in the background and an attendant read the beautiful words, with the poetry that softened the jagged edges of death.

Then the coffin was lowered into the floor, as this was to be a cremation, and Tommy got up abruptly. For a moment he stood dazed, as though he had forgotten what he was going to do. The small group of mourners, chiefly middle-aged men, filed past, pausing to shake hands and offer a few brief but genuine words of sympathy and loss and love for the dead. Among them was Clark Dixon who, after a murmured word to Tommy, drifted out of the funeral parlor. I followed him and stood blinking in the sunlight, drawing in a breath of spring air, tainted, of course, with the fumes of gasoline.

Clark, who loomed over the men who were going their separate ways, away from death and back into the reassuring routine of life, smiled at me. "I'm glad you came with Tommy. He needs your help."

"He needs yours," I told him, "as you probably know after his call yesterday."

"I'm afraid Tommy is in a nasty spot, Kate. This Summers—"

"He's horrible. I can see now how he was baiting Luisa,

suggesting that she had got out of the Waldorf by way of a freight elevator, threatening to call—I don't know whether the police or a newspaper—and she knew what he meant."

"Luisa! Luisa Hatfield?"

I nodded.

"Tommy didn't mention her when he talked to me. He just told me of the potential threat of Summers, whom he seems genuinely to believe is the killer."

"*Seems* to believe. Who else?"

Clark made no reply.

I clutched at his arm. "Don't let him down, Clark! Please don't. At this point he has a real enemy to fight."

"Tommy's worst enemy is—Tommy."

"If you won't help him, will you help me? Because, if you are right about that telephone call, Mike is involved in the Hatfield killing."

"My dear, I only suggested a possibility."

"If Tommy is right, Summers may have—done something to Mike. But Tommy wouldn't. Not Tommy."

"You and Tommy," Clark said slowly.

I held out my left hand on which I wore Allan's ring. Clark looked at it, looked at me. "Allan? So you heeded my warning, after all."

That wasn't the basis on which I wanted my engagement to Allan to rest, but before I could find the right words, Clark said uneasily, "A prompt reaction like that is enough to make any guy wonder whether he has the right to play *deus ex machina.* I'm not infallible, you know." He bent over and kissed me. "I wish you all the best, my dear."

He turned, smiling, as Tommy came out, looking from one to the other, his face like a thundercloud.

Clark said abruptly, "See you later, Kate," and went to put his hand on Tommy's arm. For a moment I thought Tommy was about to shake it off. Then he said, "Give yourself a day's vacation, Kate. You have it coming to you."

The two men walked down the street, Clark seeming to herd the smaller man along with him.

II

When Allan called later in the afternoon, he asked if I would cook dinner if he provided the steak. "If you're too tired, of course, we can go to a restaurant. I just thought—I'm in a mood for a spot of domesticity and, anyhow, we have something to celebrate, haven't we, darling?"

I tried to make the table as pretty as I could and exchanged the black dress for a green one I had knitted for myself. I did my nails and, while the polish dried, sat looking at the bright little ring on my finger. Allan's seal. His assurance that all was well.

He arrived promptly at six, bringing not only the steak but a wonderful bottle of champagne, which I put in the refrigerator while the potatoes baked. He also brought me some red tulips. "Your special flower," he said. While I arranged them in a tall vase I had brought from home, Allan hovered around, kissing my hair, the back of my neck, the tip of my nose.

I had never seen him in such an exuberant mood, never known that he had this capacity for happiness. And I had not realized how dependent he was on me for that happiness.

For his sake, so as not to dim this moment of euphoria, I said nothing of my grinding anxiety about Mike, nothing

142

about the service I had attended that morning for Mr. Eakins, nothing about the two people who had come to the office demanding Tommy and, in the man's case, at least, making threats.

I'd tasted champagne only once before in my life, when my parents had celebrated their wedding anniversary, and then I had had only a single glass. It was only when I staggered as I got up to clear the table that I realized how assiduously Allan had kept my glass filled. I clung to the back of my chair, half laughing, half ashamed. "Allan, I think I've had too much to drink."

"My fault. I should have known. Here, you sit down while I clear up this stuff and make the coffee. I'll make someone a good wife someday. You wait and see."

Over my protests he not only cleared the table but washed and put away the dishes, and then settled me on the living room couch and brought me coffee.

"Better?" he asked, when he had removed the coffee cups.

"I'm fine now." As he came toward me, a new purposefulness in his face, I said hastily, "What about the news?"

He hesitated and then swerved toward the television set, switched it on, and came back to sit beside me, his arm along the back of the couch, his fingertips touching my shoulder. "I like that dress. It's the same color as Mike's sweater, isn't it? I thought I recognized it."

"I knitted them both myself. I'm going to be a very frugal wife, Allan."

"You'll be a perfect wife, like your mother, gay and courageous and giving. But, Kate, you can't always be giving. I want you to get, too. Get a lot. I wish to heaven—" He broke off as the set warmed and the news flashed on.

143

Once more I saw a funeral, but this time from outside a cathedral. This was a very different affair from the sober service for Mr. Eakins, with its small group of genuine mourners. This time there were mobs being held back by the police. There were cameramen and men with microphones. Then people began to emerge from the great building, some with faces familiar because I had seen them so often in the news.

"Today the body of Fillmore Hatfield the Third was laid to rest in the family vault. The services were attended by several hundred mourners. Because of the mystery surrounding his death in an alley in Greenwich Village, a number of sightseers stormed the cathedral and had to be kept back forcibly by the police. The grieving widow was accompanied by her husband's closest associate, Mr. Daniel Summers, as there was no living member of the Hatfield family, which has held a prominent place in New York society, in the financial world, and in international affairs for generations.

"In an interview this morning the Police Commissioner said that measures are being taken to solve this dastardly crime, committed against one of America's finest men and greatest philanthropists.

"After the interment Mrs. Hatfield left her suite in a midtown hotel where she and her husband spent so pitifully few honeymoon days, to take up residence in the Hatfield apartment in a building long owned by the Hatfield family. She plans to remain in seclusion for a few days until she is able to plan a future—a solitary future—unlike the brilliant social life the late Mr. Hatfield had designed for her."

The curious throng had moved back on either side as the coffin, a blanket of orchids covering it, was carried out by solemn-faced, white-gloved men, and slid into the waiting hearse. A second car followed, which men packed with wreaths and sheaves of flowers. Out of the cathedral door came the widow, dripping with weeds, a black veil covering her face, one black-gloved hand resting on the arm of Dan Summers, graven-faced, in formal morning clothes, leading her solicitously to a car. As she came nearer to the cameras, one could see, even through the veil, the black hair with its soft waves, the big dark eyes, the full voluptuous mouth.

I stared at her in disbelief. That couldn't be the zombie with the dead-white face of the day before. But she resembled the ceramic portrait I had seen in Allan's apartment.

"She's the one you did that portrait of."

"Yes, didn't I tell you? Fillmore commissioned it. Rather good, I think."

The newscaster had switched to sports and Allan turned off the set.

"You know," I said, "I never knew until yesterday that it was Mr. Hatfield who set you up with a Madison Avenue display room."

"How did you find out?"

"A man named Summers. He came to the agency and he saw my ring and he asked," I broke off abruptly, "and I told him it was yours. And that's how he happened to tell me about it. Why didn't you tell me yourself, especially after I had met him?"

"I didn't know at the time," Allan said slowly. "It was a typical Hatfield trick. And yet I should have known. God knows I should have seen it! What have I got that would make a total stranger come racing over to New Jersey, offering to set me up in a big way in New York?"

145

"You have a whole lot," I said fiercely. "Don't you ever forget it. A whole lot. A great gift, Allan. And I don't see why you should mind so much that it was Mr. Hatfield who helped you."

He rubbed his hand over his forehead and I realized then how tired he looked, how drawn. I slipped my hand in his. "Don't talk about it if you don't want to. It's just that I'm interested in anything that concerns you."

"Are you? Are you really? God, I wish we could get married tomorrow and go away to the ends of the earth and just stay there, you and me."

There was the same desperate note in his voice I had heard when he first asked me to marry him. I laughed in an attempt to lighten the atmosphere. "You'd never be able to sell your ceramics that way."

"And not this way either."

"But I thought—"

"Look, Kate, you don't know what Fillmore was like. He resented Tommy and me. He felt he had to—oh, get even. That sounds ridiculous, doesn't it, a guy like Fillmore resenting someone no-account like me."

"Allan Drummond, if you say one more word like that I'll —I'll throw something at you."

He slid his arm around me, holding me closer to him, his cheek resting on my hair. "This is how it was, Kate. Summers came over to Red Bank to see me after that story appeared in the paper. I had never heard of him before, and I didn't know him from Adam, but he was plausible, apparently all steamed up about my work and its potentialities. All I needed for the 'Big Time,' and that was his expression, was the proper outlet and the right publicity. I was to have a display room on Madison Avenue. The works."

"Well, haven't you?"

"Oh, yes. Yes, indeed. But not on the first floor where I could have a window display. In a small room on a court on the top floor. You see there was no actual deception. In words, that is. Fillmore is—was always meticulous about things like that. Kept his soul nice and bright in the sight of the Lord."

"Don't be so bitter," I protested. "It's over now."

"But don't you see that I'm left with a debt to Fillmore I can never pay and yet what I got was the same old mess of pottage. He never meant me to succeed. That's the whole point. He never meant me to."

"But you will," and I tried to sound as confident as I could, "with him or without him."

Unexpectedly Allan laughed. "We'll make out," he said, and kissed me, "and when Mike gets home—"

And at last, now his dark mood had lifted, I felt that I could tell him about Clark's theory that Mike had made that call under duress.

The lines in Allan's forehead and the new lines from the corners of his mouth to his chin deepened. "It doesn't seem possible," he said at length. "I know Mike as well as anyone and he sounded in high spirits, as though he was having the time of his life. Oh, a little guilty about going off that way, without warning, but otherwise he sees the whole thing as an adventure. He's never been that far from home before, you know. To him it's the equivalent of a transcontinental trip. I don't see why your friend Clark felt justified in getting you all stirred up about what strikes me as a screwy theory. I've been checking on him, Kate. Apparently he was quite a big

147

wheel during the war, but private sleuthing isn't on the same level, you know. There are rumors that he's as anxious as the next man to make a quick buck."

It didn't sound like Clark. Or did it? He himself had agreed that his job had its sordid aspects. He had said that he liked Tommy as a bar companion or someone with whom to go on the town. He had that big, open manner I instinctively trusted, though my father had warned me about my tendency to oversimplify. Even a coin had two sides, he had reminded me.

"Then you honestly feel that Mike is all right?"

"If he was being coerced into talking to me as he did," Allan said slowly, "he would have found some way to tip me off. He's smart as a whip, you know that. He could have said something I'd know wasn't true. There are a dozen ways he could have done it."

"Well—" As always when I was with Allan, I began to feel better, more secure.

"And he said it would be only a few days. Maybe tomorrow. Certainly the next day. And when he gets back, I'll tan his hide for him." Allan drew me closer to him and I rested my head on his shoulder.

"What would I do without you, Allan? I was getting into a worse panic than ever, thinking that Summers—"

"Summers!"

I told him the theory that Summers and Luisa between them had planned the murder and that she had promised to marry him and share the wealth, and then turned against him.

"Summers!" Allan said incredulously. "Summers! And Luisa." He turned to cup my face in his hands, looking

148

steadily into my eyes. "If you've got any idea like that, for God's sake don't speak of it to anyone. It's dynamite. Do you realize that? And where on earth could you have made any connection between them?"

"When they both came to the office yesterday," I said, and saw the naked shock in his face. "Only, of course, I didn't know that it was Luisa. She said she was Mrs. Stevenson and she looked awful, like a zombie, with a blond wig and a dead-white face. But the Summers man came in and they talked and I didn't understand until later what they were talking about when I found out who she was."

"How did you find out?"

"Tommy. Calling herself Mrs. Stevenson and they were living under the name of J. Hyde, *Dr. Jekyll and Mr. Hyde,* you know. And Summers is going to try to throw all the blame on Tommy, because he saw Luisa is interested in him."

"Tommy! You say he didn't get home until after the police had removed his father's body and Fillmore must have been killed somewhere about that time. How do you know when Tommy really got home?" When I made no reply, he asked, "How do you know? Why haven't you told the police Fillmore came to the office? Are you covering for Tommy?" His voice changed. "Forgive me, darling. That was inexcusable. You're the last girl in the world to do a thing like that. Look here, you've got to get out of this place. It isn't safe for you. I wish to God we could be married at once, but we'll have to wait for a couple of months until the money starts coming in. But at least I can find you another place to live until we can be together. Forever."

149

It was all my fault, I thought miserably, after Allan had gone. With the best intentions in the world I had managed, in my own inimitable way, to convince him not of Summers's guilt, but of Tommy's. I turned Allan's ring round and round on my finger. At least I could not say I had not been warned. There was Clark's warning; and, from the beginning, Allan had not trusted Tommy; and, according to the Summers man, he was an inveterate girl-chaser. Then why, I asked myself in a rage, didn't it make any difference? The only way I'd ever be safe from Tommy would be by marrying Allan now, before there was any perilous delay.

And, thinking only of myself, I even forgot Mike that night.

But the next morning my fear was back again, as sharp and deep as ever. It was Thursday and he had been gone six days.

I unlocked the agency, opened the windows to let out the stale air, took yesterday's letters from the mailboxes, and I had barely started to open them when the door opened and Biddy Blanchard came in. As usual she looked as though she had flung her clothes on in the dark. And as usual she looked enchanting.

"Kate!" She came to fling her arms around me and give me a kiss. "News from Mike!"

"Mike!"

She nodded vigorously and sat on the chair beside my desk, pawing frantically through an immense handbag. "I've got it somewhere. Oh, here it is! We came home late last night and never thought of looking for mail until this morning."

Triumphantly she held out a shipping tag reading, "Mr. Joe Blanchard," with the Village address. Attached to the metal tag was what appeared to be a small whistle.

I looked at it and then looked at her. Then I looked at the address again. It was Mike's writing! And the postmark was dated Monday in New York City.

"Well?" Biddy demanded, her small, piquant face alive with eagerness.

"It's a dog whistle. Mike bought it out of his allowance for Joe's birthday because of the new dog."

"And I can tell you one thing, Kate. Joe did not make a threatening call to you about Mike. He was sick when I asked him about it—sick that I'd suspect him of a thing like that."

Feet clattered on the stairs and Tommy came in, glanced at Biddy, said "Good morning," and started toward the inner office.

"Tommy, wait!" When he had come back, brows arched in a question, I said, "Biddy, this is Tommy Eakins, my boss. Mrs. Blanchard, Tommy."

She held out her hand with the spontaneous warmth that always attracted people, and Tommy smiled down at her.

"Biddy brought me this." I held out the dog whistle and explained that Mike had bought it for Joe and that it had been mailed in New York on Monday.

"Are you sure this is your brother's writing?"

"Positive."

"So now we know that phone call from Rochester was phony and he has been here in New York all the time."

"But he didn't call until after Monday."

"Then where was he from the time when he disappeared on Saturday morning until he mailed this in New York on

Monday? The Rochester story still doesn't hold up, unless he made that call under pressure, as Clark suggested."

"I see that. What am I going to do, Tommy?"

Biddy looked quickly from me to Tommy, a little smile curving her lips.

"I don't know. I'm fresh out of ideas, which seems to be my normal state. I'll get hold of Clark at once. But what I can't see is how, if Mike was able to put this in a mailbox, he wasn't able to get to a telephone. That is, if he was a free agent."

"Suppose," Biddy said in her light, quick voice, "Mike wasn't free to mail it. Suppose he had this in his pocket and dropped it out of a car or threw it out of a window and someone else picked it up and mailed it."

"That's a lot of ifs," Tommy told her, smiling. "But it's as good a theory as any that Kate or I have produced."

"But at least," I held onto the one thing I was sure of, "we know he was alive when he called Allan and that was after this was mailed."

"The problem, dear," Tommy said gently, unaware of his use of the endearment, "is that Mike might have dropped the thing any time from Saturday morning on; someone might have picked it up and carried it around absent-mindedly for a couple of days before mailing it."

"You might advertise for anyone who found and mailed it," Biddy suggested. "At least you'd know where it was found, if that is what happened to it."

"But that might take days," I wailed, "and the one who found it might not read the ads, and—"

"Summers!" Tommy said abruptly. "If this is Summers's work, I'll break his neck."

"Tommy!" I nearly shouted, but at least I stopped him on his way out. "Don't do anything like that on your own. Call Clark. Please call Clark."

"Suppose," Tommy said in the tone of a boss addressing an insubordinate subordinate, "you let me handle my own affairs, Miss Forbes."

When he had gone, I blinked at Biddy, who shook her head. "Men!" she said. "Don't look so stricken, Kate. It's just a phase they go through when they get into a state over a girl. Like having to stand on their heads and turn somersaults when they are twelve. They grow out of it—as a rule."

When she had gone, leaving the dog whistle on the desk before me, I called Clark, but I got an answering service to take my number and a message to call back. It was vital. What I hoped, of course, was that Clark would be able to sidetrack Tommy before he could tangle with Summers and do something violent.

Then I called the number of Allan's Madison Avenue shop and was told by a polite young man that Mr. Drummond was making deliveries and would not be back all day.

I'd never been more frustrated. I held the tag of the dog whistle tight in my hand, my only link to Mike, which might mean he was alive and well or might mean nothing at all except that his Rochester call had been an act of coercion.

When the telephone rang, I answered dully, "Eakins Travel Agency."

A low sexy voice said, "I'd like to speak to Mr. Eakins, please. This is Mrs. Stevenson calling."

"He's not here, Mrs. Stevenson."

"You're lying!" And her voice wasn't sexy at all.

"He's not here, Mrs. Hatfield."

Twelve

There was a long pause and then Luisa Hatfield said, "Look here, Assistant, I think it is time we had a little talk."

"I can't imagine why."

She laughed. "Get off your tail and get up here. If you know who I am, you know the address. I'll tell them I'm expecting you."

"I don't—"

"Are you interested in seeing Mike again?"

"I'm coming," I said, and she laughed again.

I left a sign, "Back in an hour," on the door and locked it. I almost ran on my way to the subway, plunged down the dark stairs, and waited impatiently while the train streaked along the platform and jolted to a stop. At this time of day there were empty seats and I sat staring at an advertisement for shampoo all the way up to Seventy-seventh Street.

Moving from a byway in the Village to the great sweep of Fifth Avenue with the park stretching along one side and the soaring luxury apartment buildings on the other was like moving into another world. It not only looked different, with the greenery and budding forsythia, with riders silhouetted against the skyline as they rode in Central Park, with uniformed doormen standing under canopies, but it smelled better. A lot better.

It was only after I had verified the number and walked past a sharp-eyed doorman into the Hatfield Building that I realized, partly from his expression, partly from my surroundings, that my shabby spring coat, now entering its third season, my homemade dress, my hair which I had set myself, were badly out of place.

A man at a desk raised disapproving eyebrows until I said, "Mrs. Hatfield, please. I am expected."

"Name?"

I was tempted to say *Assistant*. "Katherine Forbes."

"Oh, yes, Mrs. Hatfield is expecting you. The elevator on your left."

The elevator operator also gave me a quick look, summing up the kind of person the new Mrs. Hatfield entertained. It wasn't, clearly, what the management was accustomed to.

"I'm afraid I don't know the number."

"The fifteenth floor," he said loftily, and the cage rose in silence. There was a velvet-covered seat and the walls were mirror-lined so, before it came to a smooth stop, I saw a lot of glimpses of a small red-haired girl in a shabby brown coat.

There was a table, another mirror, and a vase of flowers in the hallway and a single door which stood open. The butler said, "Miss Forbes? This way, please." Through an arch I could see a drawing room that looked out on Fifth Avenue from half a dozen long windows. On either side of it wide arches opened into other rooms, the one on the left apparently a library, the one on the right a formal dining

155

room. But we did not go through the great drawing room. The butler led me along a corridor with half a dozen doors to the one at the end, on which he tapped. It was opened by a uniformed maid.

"Miss Forbes to see Mrs. Hatfield," the butler said.

"Mrs. Hatfield is expecting Miss Forbes."

All at once I was shaken by giggles, remembering the immortal exchange: "For the Duchess. An invitation from the Queen to play croquet." "From the Queen. An invitation to the Duchess to play croquet." As a result, I forgot my nervousness and my sense of inadequacy as I went into the little morning room where Luisa Hatfield was lying on a chaise longue, wearing the most revealing housecoat I had ever seen, and, I'll have to admit, the most devastatingly becoming. She did not need to fear the morning light that struck her face. She was really beautiful, not only the body she took such shameless pride in revealing, but her face with its immense, dark, heavy-lidded eyes and the sensuous mouth. A greedy mouth and discontented eyes. But she was loving her surroundings, the luxury—loving every minute of it. I knew then that Tommy was probably right. She had an innate toughness that would make the inherent violence in Summers seem ineffectual. In her he had more than met his match. If anyone had instigated the murder of her husband, it was this woman, and the man had merely served as her tool.

She noticed my swift look around me at a kind of luxury I had never seen except in old movies, in which even secretaries apparently lived in a state of splendor unknown since the days of the Sun King. She motioned me to a chair, satin-covered and beautifully carved, with a gesture that set the

156

diamond on her finger flashing like a headlight.

"It's a far cry from the Village, isn't it?" she said in amusement.

"And from Hoboken," I answered sweetly.

Unexpectedly she laughed. "You're a little scrapper, aren't you, Assistant?"

"Only if I have to be. What do you want of me, Mrs. Hatfield?"

"What makes you think I want anything?"

"I can't imagine you doing anything unless you expected to gain by it."

This time she did not laugh. Her lower lip thrust out in an odd way and her teeth nibbled at the inside while she studied me. "All right," she said at last, "how much do you want?"

I blinked at her in sheer astonishment. "I don't know what you are talking about."

"Don't take that tone with me, Assistant! I'm holding all the cards. The sooner you realize that, the better off you'll be."

"I don't know what kind of hand you think you have, but you'd better not stake too much on it. You've got only one thing I want."

Her lips twitched with amusement, but she said gravely, "And what is that?"

"Mike."

Her eyes widened. She was completely taken aback and so was I. There had been only one reason why I had agreed to see her—Mike—and she wasn't even thinking of him. But if that was the case, why had she used his name to get me here?

"This morning," she said, and her voice was harsh,

"Tommy beat up Dan Summers, claiming that he had abducted your brother Mike. Dan knows nothing about the kid. Neither do I. But it seemed the best way of getting you here."

"What do you want with me?"

"I want Tommy. All my life I've got what I wanted in the long run and I don't intend to miss out now. And you aren't going to get in my way. Dan sized you up right away as bad news. I want you to clear out of that office tomorrow and I don't care what excuse you give. I'll pay you twenty-five thousand dollars as soon as I can get my hands on some of the Hatfield money, because I'll have only a widow's allowance until Filly's estate is settled."

Filly! Again I was so shaken by giggles that it was difficult to control myself and she saw it, bewildered by my change of attitude.

"You'd better think of it. Tommy can't give you that much in years, not with that crummy agency. In fact, he'll probably have to shut up shop any day now and go on unemployment unless he sees things the way they are."

"Look here," I said, feeling rather sorry for her, "you couldn't be more mistaken."

"What about?"

"About everything. In the first place, I'm not making a play for Tommy, whatever Summers may say. I'm engaged to someone else." I held out my hand with its tiny diamond. "A man named Allan Drummond."

"Drummond!"

"Oh, that's right. You know him. He did a ceramic portrait of you. I've seen it in his apartment."

"So you are going to marry Allan Drummond. Well, well.

The best of luck to you, Assistant. When's the happy event to be?"

"Not long, but Allan has to wait for some money to come in."

Again her teeth worried the underskin of her lip. "And in the meantime you'll be brightening up Tommy's office. Is that the plan?"

I got up. "If that's all you want of me—"

Her hand darted out like a striking snake and she seized my wrist, pushed me back in the chair. "Not so fast. How did you know who I was?"

"J. Hyde. Stevenson. Tommy got it at once, though he didn't recognize my description of you."

She laughed at that. "I should hope not."

"But when I told him that you and Summers knew each other and that he was needling you, really threatening you—"

"You told Tommy that?" At the blaze of rage in her eyes I found myself pushing back in my chair. "What did Tommy say?"

"He said," I told her with satisfaction, " 'what a fool that woman is!' And I can tell you this, Mrs. Hatfield, Tommy Eakins wouldn't have you at any price. And if you and your friend Summers had anything to do with Mike's disappearance or you are setting Tommy up as a patsy, you'll be sorry you were ever born."

"Oh, for God's sake, what interest would we have in your brother?"

"We think he saw Mr. Hatfield's murder and that's why he was abducted. And if anything happens to him, Mrs. Hatfield, you and Summers will go to prison for it."

159

"Dan—and I?" She got up. "Wait a minute. I'll be back."

I thought of leaving but I waited, hoping, after all, to get some hint about Mike. She was back within a few minutes, and returned to the chaise longue, lighting a cigarette, the great diamond on her finger flashing with multi-colored lights as she did so, the lines of her body clearly revealed by that almost transparent housecoat, under which she wore nothing at all.

"Now then, Assistant, let's have this story about Dan and me being sent to prison. Just lay it on the line, sister."

So I told her that her husband had been found in the alley beside the agency, which meant someone knew he intended to go there, and the murder had been done at that particular spot to point the finger at Tommy.

"But I never—but that—" She stopped.

"And Mike disappeared just about the time of the murder. So I believe Summers took him away and then he was jealous of Tommy, so that's why the murder was done that way."

"Tommy! Why, you little fool—"

"I know. You never meant it to happen like that, did you? I think you meant to double-cross Summers and, instead, he double-crossed you."

"So you think Dan killed Filly. Now that's a thought." She was mocking me now.

"If he was so innocent—and if you were—why was he trying to hold you up for money while you were both at the agency? Now he knows you prefer Tommy he's going to salvage what he can. He even expects to get a cut after Tommy marries you. Except that he won't. Not ever."

"You're sure of that, aren't you?"

I nodded. "And if anything happens to Tommy because of

you or Summers, you'll have me to fight all the way."

"It strikes me that Drummond is getting a damned poor bargain in you." Luisa stood up, her white flesh lovely and shimmering through the transparent robe. "Get out, Assistant! You're trying to play in the big league and you're only little-league caliber. Don't forget that."

I went out of the room and down the long corridor. At the far end a door stood open and I saw a chef in his high white hat. Through another open door I saw a maid running a vacuum cleaner. The butler was not in sight and I let myself out and rang for the elevator. I found that I was trembling —a long slow tremor that shook my whole body. But whether it was reaction or fear, I didn't know.

The lobby was luxurious, with shaded lights, deep chairs and couches, and a carpet into which my feet sank. I went out of the dimness into the bright light. The doorman was helping a woman into a cab. As I started down the Avenue, a hand closed over my elbow and Dan Summers fell into step beside me. He was not his usual well-groomed self. His collar was rumpled, there was a rip in the seam of his coat sleeve, a big red swelling on his jaw, and one eye was beginning to turn black.

"Well," I said brightly, "apparently Tommy managed to find you."

I'll never learn! For a moment all the violence inherent in the man seemed to leap to the surface, but he managed to smile, though apparently it hurt his bruised mouth. He paused beside a big Lincoln, unlocked the door and pushed me inside. As I resisted, he twisted my arm brutally so that I whimpered with pain.

"One sound out of you, sister, and I'll give you just the

161

kind of beating Eakins gave me. I mean that. I have no soft spot in my heart for little redheads."

For once I was cowed enough to keep still. Not exactly frightened. I didn't believe in the beating and I didn't see what he could do to me. Or why. All I wished was that I had been able to get hold of Allan that morning. Allan would know what to do. Allan would keep me safe.

Dan slid under the wheel and the big car slid noiselessly into traffic. The fact that he had not taken time to clean himself up or change his coat meant that Luisa had sent out an S O S for him to pick me up when I left her apartment. So at last I knew beyond doubt of the connection between Summers and Luisa. Tommy had been right about that.

Summers turned left into Central Park and drove down to Columbus Circle, fed into the converging lines into Broadway, down to Forty-eighth Street, turned into an underground parking space where he took a ticket and ordered me out with a duck of his head. All the way downtown I was thinking that the trunk of a car like that could easily hold a small boy.

Because of that steel hand on my wrist, I accompanied Summers into a big, dingy, cheap hotel. The people in the lobby looked, even to my untutored eyes, like actors either on their way up or on their way down. Certainly they did not have it made as of now. The carrying voices, the careful diction, the gestures that were larger than life-size, the copies of *Variety*, the discussions of casting and Equity and the general stinkingness of producers was going on all around me. One very old man held what was obviously a book of clippings, aged and yellow, and I felt a pang of pity for him. Actors often make such terrific sums of money and almost never manage to hold onto any of it.

There was an ancient open-cage elevator with a sign "Out of Order," which apparently had been hanging there for a long time. Anyhow, Summers automatically turned to the stairs.

I balked. "Where are you taking me?"

"To my rooms where we can talk. I have no designs on you, baby. Don't fear a fate worse than death. And save your breath. We have six flights to climb."

With that iron hand never releasing its grip, we went up the six flights of stairs. I don't remember seeing anyone in all that time except for a sloppy woman in a dirty dress pushing a broom along a corridor and a girl with too much makeup who passed us running down.

She waved at Summers. "They're casting for *Winter Magic.*"

"Good luck. I'll keep my fingers crossed," he called cheerfully and I realized that in the dim light she had not observed his battered appearance.

Evidently he was accustomed to the climb because he was not even out of breath when we reached the top floor, though I was panting and my knees were trembling from the unaccustomed strain. I'd never climbed that many stairs in my life.

At the end of the hall he unlocked a door and stood back to let me precede him. I was surprised. Whatever I had expected in this run-down old building, it was not a comfortable, well-furnished suite of rooms: a large living room with windows opening on Forty-eighth Street, a comfortable bedroom, a neat bath, compact kitchenette behind folding doors which now stood open. You could see everything in the

163

apartment at a glance. There were a few jarring notes: a small chair had been overturned and a table, its lamp a broken heap on the carpet, and the floor strewn with cigarette butts from a broken ash tray. I could not help looking at these signs of combat with open pleasure.

Dan Summers's big smile was missing now. Deliberately he locked the door and put the key in his pocket. Then he went to the telephone and said, "I'll be out of town for several days. Please hold any messages until I call for them. Okay?"

Then he came back, settled himself comfortably, and waved me carelessly to a chair. I shook my head. He shrugged. "Suit yourself. But understand one thing. Tommy Eakins went berserk this morning and tried to take me apart."

"It looks as though he had succeeded," I said cordially.

"No one does that to me and gets away with it. You are now going to call him and tell him that you are permanently out of circulation unless he gives me a written confession that he killed Hatfield. When I get that, and only when I get that, you'll go free. And I won't use it unless he forces my hand. That all clear?"

"You're just plain stupid. Tommy didn't kill Hatfield and you know it. If he gets a message like that from me, he'll call the police at once and tell them just what he knows about you and Luisa. And I can tell you another thing. If you are hoping to keep Luisa in the clear so she can collect Hatfield money to share with you, you're mistaken. And if you try to do anything to me, Tommy will finish the job he began this morning."

Summers got up in a leisurely way, slapped me savagely

164

across the face, knocking my head against the back of the chair, and resumed his seat. "Just a sample."

"I can't wait to see what happens next time Tommy gets to work on you."

He smiled, though I could see with considerable satisfaction that it hurt his mouth and started his lip bleeding. He dabbed at the cut with his handkerchief.

"For heaven's sake, don't use that!" I exclaimed. "The thing is filthy. You could get a bad infection that way."

He looked at the handkerchief, looked at me, and laughed. "I'll be damned!" Then he went into his bathroom and came out with a handful of clean tissues. "So you think I'm the type to live on women," he said. He hadn't liked the idea— at least not when it was put into words. "With a car like mine? With this apartment?" There was bitterness in his voice.

"Oh," I exclaimed, enlightened, "of course. One of Mr. Hatfield's tricks. A big car, a comfortable apartment, but a lousy building and—I'll bet—low pay. And the chances are he owns this building."

"The girl has brains as well as good looks. We must get to know each other better."

"Not a chance."

"Because of Tommy?"

"You seem to forget Allan. Anyhow, I've found out one thing. Aside from wanting Hatfield's wife and his money, you also resented him, didn't you?" I insisted, "Didn't you? He kept you short and kept you grateful. The Hatfield syndrome."

"My, my, what a big word for a little girl."

"Let me go, Mr. Summers. It's no use keeping me here.

165

I warn you right now that Tommy won't stand for it."

He fingered the sore spot on his jaw, pondering. Abruptly he asked, "And what about Mike?" He laughed at my expression. "You seem to have forgotten about Mike."

There was a sudden banging on the door. We both jumped. Summers waved for me to keep quiet. There was another barrage of bangs, as though someone was pounding with clenched fists. "Open up there! Lemme in, Dan'l. I just want to have one li'l drink with Dan'l. Dan'l in the lion's den. A lion in Dan'l's den. Come on, open up. I saw your li'l redhead, Dan'l. Don't be selfish." The barrage began again.

"Damn him to hell," Summers said under his breath. He dragged me across the room to the bathroom, took the key from inside the door and pushed me in, locking the door behind me. "One sound out of you and I'll beat the daylights out of you. I'll spoil your pretty looks for Tommy. I mean Allan."

I heard Summers open the outside door. "Cut out that racket and go sleep it off, whoever you are. You're drunk as a coot. Cut along now."

"Just one drink first," the drunk said cajolingly. "Finished my last bottle and my credit's no good." He had trouble with his words. "No good. Won't sell me a single bottle on credit. So you won't refuse one drink. Good neighbor policy."

I could hear a chair creak as he settled himself, apparently impervious to Summer's fury. "Just one drink. Now where's the girl?"

I banged on the bathroom door and shouted, "Let me out! Let me out!"

There was a moment's silence and then the drunk laughed. "Now that's not right. Let the little girl out. She can have

166

a drink with us. Come on, Dan. Let her out."

"Mind your own business and get out of here! Go take a cold shower and sober up."

"All right, but let the girl out first. I won't go until she's out." He said then, in a different tone, "I'm in no hurry, no hurry at all, Summers. Let the girl go now," and he had sobered up in a rush.

"Who are you?"

"Take your choice of names. It's all the same to me. But I want to see that girl walk out safe and sound."

Summers opened the door and I ran past him—past the drunk who was not a drunk, and out of the room, hurtling down the long flight of stairs into the street.

Thirteen

The sign was off the agency door and Tommy was sitting in the outer office. Before I got inside, he was across the floor and I was in his arms, clinging to him, shaking. He held me, not speaking, except for a low murmur of foolish endearments that meant nothing but were comforting.

At last his words became more coherent. "What happened to you? Where have you been? What happened?"

"That," Allan said from the doorway, "is a good question."

Very gently Tommy released me. Allan's face was working with fury, but Tommy seemed to be in complete control of himself. "I'm glad you're here, Allan. This girl seems to need you."

"I'm glad to hear it," Allan said dryly.

Tommy ignored Allan's rage. "She just came in, as though all the furies were after her, and nearly shaking herself apart with nerves. I've been trying to find out what is wrong, what happened to her?"

Allan came then to put his arm around me. "Sorry I lost

my temper, darling. What's wrong?"

At first, trying to tell everything at once, I was so incoherent that I merely bewildered them. Then I shook my head, trying to clear it, and sat down, clasping my hands, took three long breaths and then told them what had happened, beginning, for Allan's benefit, with Biddy Blanchard bringing the dog whistle Mike had managed in some way to get to Joe, a sign that he was alive and somewhere in New York.

"For God's sake!" Allan exclaimed. "For God's sake! Why didn't you let me know at once?"

"I tried to reach you and to reach Clark, but I couldn't. And then," I went on to Luisa's call. She had asked for Tommy, saying she was Mrs. Stevenson, and when I had said he was not in she called me a liar, so I had said, "He's not in, Mrs. Hatfield."

"Oh, no, Kate!" Allan protested.

"Oh, Kate, you little donkey," Tommy said at the same time, and they exchanged glances of mutual bafflement and despair.

"So then," I said, "she told me to get up to the Hatfield apartment at once and when I refused, she said I'd better, if I wanted to see Mike alive."

Again the two men exclaimed in unison.

So I described that interview with Luisa and how she had claimed I was after Tommy and I'd said I was engaged to Allan. Again the two men reacted in the same way, but they did not speak, they simply looked at each other.

"She offered me twenty-five thousand dollars to get out of the agency and leave Tommy alone. So I told her if anything happened to Mike, I'd see that she and Summers went to prison for it."

169

By now Tommy and Allan were acting like Tweedledum and Tweedledee. They exchanged gloomy looks and heaved deep sighs. I could have banged their heads together.

But when I described leaving the building, where Summers was waiting for me, and how he had forced me into his car and taken me to his hotel, they dropped the comedy routine. With an exclamation Allan cupped my chin in his hand and turned my face to the light. "How did you get that mark on your cheek, Kate?"

"He struck me. He said if I got out of line, he'd do to me what Tommy had done to him."

"But what on earth did he want of you?" Allan exclaimed.

"He wanted me to call Tommy and say he'd take me out of circulation permanently unless Tommy produced a written confession that he had killed Hatfield."

"What!" Again the two men spoke in unison.

"He promised that if he got the confession he would let me go and he'd never use it unless Tommy forced him to."

Allan held my hand in a tight clasp. "I don't see, Tommy, why the hell this girl has to be involved in your affairs."

"I think Summers has Mike," I said. "We've got to save Mike."

"How did you get away?" Tommy asked.

"Well, that was one of those incredibly lucky breaks," I said.

Clark came in and gave me a long, searching look. He expelled a little sigh of relief. "So you're all right."

"Yes, but how did you know?"

Clark grinned. "Well, you left a fairly frantic message at my answering service but not very clear. As soon as I was free from another job, I came to find out what you wanted."

170

"I'll give you the background later. I've just told it to Allan and Tommy. But the thing is that I was abducted by Summers this afternoon and taken to his hotel. And he threatened to take me out of circulation, where I think he has hidden Mike, until he got a written confession from Tommy that he had killed Hatfield."

"My, my," Clark said so calmly that I could have shaken him. "What will people think of next?"

"It isn't funny. And if it hadn't been for some incredible luck, a drunk banging at the door and demanding a drink and refusing to go away unless Summers produced the red-headed girl, I don't know what would have happened. Tommy had to let him in because he was making—"

"Why not stop for breath?" Clark suggested.

I ignored that. "Anyhow Summers had to let me go after I shouted, and so I ran and that is all."

Allan put his arm around me. "What an unspeakable thing! This settles it, Kate. You've got to get out of this place before Tommy involves you in any more trouble."

"I think you are right about that," Tommy said. "I've given her the same advice."

"The beauty of this story," Clark said in that gentle voice, though this time tinged with laughter, "is the incredible luck that brought the drunk to Summers's door in the nick of time."

"Clark! You knew about him!"

He laughed. "Of course I did. He's been following Summers ever since I began looking into things. Quite an eventful day Summers must have spent," and he gave Tommy an amused look. "Summers could have given you a good fifteen pounds, too. That must have been quite a scrap! I didn't know you had it in you."

"I didn't either," Tommy admitted candidly. "But the idea that Mike was being held captive somewhere—"

"I seem to have missed the boat," Allan said, "but I don't understand why you've had a man trailing Dan Summers."

"So you suspected him, all the time." Tommy sounded gratified.

"Actually, I never was so surprised in my life," Clark admitted. "I'd been building a different theory. Quite a different theory."

"But at last we know for sure about the link between Luisa and Summers," I said. "And Summers hated Hatfield, if you need another motive beside Luisa and her money. He hated him the way Allan and Tommy do because he never meant Summers to get anywhere. I suppose because he's so devastatingly handsome that Hatfield liked putting him off in that old hotel and I'll bet he couldn't even get gas for that Lincoln except with a credit card Hatfield got for him. You know, I don't think Hatfield is going to be missed very much."

"Exit with hollow laughter," Tommy said. "So we are three men in the same boat."

"And the boat wasn't seaworthy," Allan commented.

Clark grunted. "I've been looking at Hatfield's will, though I had a bit of time getting anyone to divulge. Oddly enough, about the only person who will be satisfied with his cut will be Summers. He gets a cool hundred thousand as a token of gratitude to a faithful friend."

"But what about Luisa?" Allan demanded.

Clark chuckled. "She gets two-thirds of the whole estate."

"Good God! What would she expect? Fort Knox?"

Clark threw back his head and laughed delightedly, laughter that was infectious. "A typical Hatfield trick. Strings attached. 'To protect my beloved wife from being victimized by fortune hunters I am appointing the trustees listed below to administer Mrs. Hatfield's estate, paying her the sum of thirty thousand dollars a year until she is sixty, at which time the capital will come to her in its entirety.' Typical, isn't it? If he isn't around to enjoy his wife, she won't enjoy his money, but she'll never be able to forget that it is there, just out of reach."

After a pause while we digested the information, Allan turned to Clark. "Let's get back to the main point. What do you think, Dixon? We can't take any more chances with Kate. But what about Mike?"

Clark made one of his oblique answers. "I want Mike alive. I'm willing to give up a lot for that."

II

Well, at least we knew now. Summers and Luisa had planned the murder, and Summers had carried it out, witnessed by Mike. Someone had planned things so that Tommy would be blamed. Now he would learn that, even if Luisa could be brought to marry him, there would be little of the Hatfield money to be had through her.

There seemed to be nothing to say at the moment. After Clark had said he wanted Mike alive he took his departure. Allan gave me a quick kiss and left for his display room where, apparently, he expected some buyers whom the salesman could not handle alone.

"You go home," Tommy told me. "You've had enough for one day. More than enough. If I could tell you how sorry—

173

how terribly sorry I am about this, Kate—"

"But it's not your fault."

"Isn't it?" He reached for his lightweight topcoat and shrugged into it. "I'll close the agency. And, for God's sake, be sure your door is locked."

III

And then it was Friday morning. I came out of a heavy sleep to shut off the alarm. I'd forgotten some of the horror until, out of habit, I went to Mike's door and remembered that he was gone. He had been missing seven days.

When I started to wash my face, I noticed that one cheek was still reddened, with two dark fingerprints where Dan had struck me. And Mike was in the hands of a man like that— a violent man.

The sign was still on the agency door, which meant that Tommy had not returned to the office. There were some letters and a few bills. The business letters I was able to answer myself, and I put my answers on his desk for his signature, along with the sheaf of bills.

It was eleven when Tommy came down. It didn't take more than one look to learn that he had been drinking heavily. It had obviously been a hard night. His eyes were bloodshot.

He stood in the doorway, looking at me. "Good morning," he said curtly, and went past me to his own office.

At noon I spread out my package of sandwiches and thermos of coffee on a clean paper towel. I had just unwrapped a tunafish sandwich when Clark came in, following his knock —a grave Clark, more serious than I had ever seen him.

174

Only one thought leaped to my mind. "Mike! Have you heard anything about Mike?"

"I've had a talk with the police. A long talk. After hearing about Summers."

Tommy flung open the door of the inner office. "What has Summers done?"

"It's what has been done to Summers," Clark said. "I slipped up badly or my man did. Dan Summers was found shot to death in his apartment at that old hotel at five o'clock this morning. An elderly character actress who is 'resting' has a room next to his. She heard the sound of a shot and reported it to the desk, but they didn't take it seriously because she is always reporting something wrong and anyhow Summers had informed the desk that he would be out of town for a few days."

Clark was taking his time, looking from Tommy to me; the manner that was always so open was now restrained. Tommy began to drum his fingers on the desk and, at last, as though he could not help it, reached for his case and lighted the first cigarette of the day, the match shaking so he had difficulty in making it connect.

"Well," Clark went on, after tension had been stretched to the breaking point, and I was ready to cry out, "the woman waited for what seemed to her a reasonable time and when nothing happened, she called the desk again. She told the night clerk that unless he investigated within twenty minutes, and she was going to time him, she was going to call the police herself.

"Now hotels, even that kind, perhaps especially that kind, don't take kindly to the incursion of New York's Finest, so the poor guy trundled up six flights of stairs—no wonder

175

Summers kept in such good shape!—and opened the door with his master key. And there, sure enough, was Summers, shot to death while he lay in bed."

Tommy was smoking with nervous jerks, beating a tattoo on the desk, and Clark stood leaning against the wall, hands relaxed at his sides, his good-humored face hard and set.

"When the police arrived, the old actress, Gladys Golding, remember her? She did revivals of *Arsenic and Old Lace* and *Kind Lady* a few years ago. Naturally she has her eye on some free publicity. She could use it, poor thing."

"You've seen her?" Tommy said oddly.

"Yes. Actually I've just come from there. She had quite a story. She had not only heard the shot that killed Dan Summers—"

"Could it have been suicide, if he knew how he had lost out all along the line?" Tommy asked.

"Shot himself in the head with his hands under the covers? Hardly. He seems to have been asleep, facing the wall, and literally never knew what hit him. Unless, of course, he was a sleight-of-hand artist. Well, as I say, aside from the fatal shot, the old lady had heard a lot during the day. First someone had a terrible fight with Summers, knocking furniture around, shouting, all that. She didn't see who that was and she couldn't be sorrier at having missed anything.

"Somewhat later on in this eventful day, someone banged on Summers's door and shouted, making a terrible racket. She was just about to call the desk and complain about the noise when the man shouted something about a redhead and Summers admitted his determined visitor, who appeared to be drunk. Drunk and disorderly. She left the door open in case it was the other man back for a fight. She explained that

176

there was a limit to what anyone was expected to put up with, and though Mr. Summers was a nice-looking gentleman, and knew it too, he'd have been fine in one of those old Clark Gable parts, you can't expect anyone to put up with such goings-on.

"So a little later Summer's door was flung open and a girl came running out and tore down the stairs as though she expected to be pursued. The old lady has good eyes as well as good hearing. She described the girl as not more than sixteen, small, red-haired, very pretty, very frightened."

In the silence that followed, my thoughts were noisy. At last I said, "But you knew all that yesterday, Clark. You knew Tommy and I had been there and why it had happened."

He nodded. "It's a question of motive. Can't you see that? If Summers locked you up, threatening you, and you escaped by a miracle, you might want to get even."

"Are you saying," and I tried to laugh, "that I shot Summers last night? I couldn't kill anyone. I don't own a gun and I wouldn't know how to use it if I did."

"You just aim it and pull the trigger."

"But even if I could do that, I wouldn't. I didn't. Because he's the only link I have to Mike and now no one can tell me where he is."

Clark took out a pipe and packed it slowly, his attention apparently focused on what he was doing. "You see, little Kate, that was a good description the actress furnished the police."

"But there must be a lot of red-haired girls in New York. There's no possible way she could identify me."

"But there's Luisa. According to you, she set you up yesterday, and I can't see her holding back a trump card like that."

"But I wasn't in that hotel last night," I said stubbornly. "I was right downstairs in my apartment."

"Alone, of course. Not a very good alibi."

"She doesn't need an alibi," Tommy said roughly. "Damn it, Kate, you should have run off and married Allan at once."

"What about you, Tommy?" Clark asked as though he had just thought of it. "What's your alibi?"

The color drained out of Tommy's face as he stared at him. The hand holding the cigarette shook. "I don't have one. Last night I got drunk as a coot. I don't know where I went or what time I got home—or how. I just fell across the bed and went to sleep without undressing."

"No alibi," Clark said, "and, God knows, plenty of motive."

"As you know damned well," Tommy said through set teeth.

I hadn't taken seriously the idea that I might be accused of killing Dan Summers, but this was different. This was Tommy and he was cornered. I leaped to his assistance like a tigress protecting its young.

"What's wrong with you this morning, Clark? What makes you think Tommy and I are the only people who could have killed Summers? What about Luisa? They may have been partners once, but they weren't when I saw them."

To my relief Clark smiled approvingly. "You have a point there. A guy I knew in the service who's with the police department—actually he's the one who is responsible for my present job—was in the Summers apartment when I got

178

there. He let me hang around while they were searching the place. I glanced over some letters on Summers's desk, and guess what?"

"Leave us not be pixie," Tommy said, his voice on edge.

Clark ignored that. "I'm the careful type, see all, hear all, say nuffin'. Anyhow, in an envelope with the printed address of Common Cause, I found, instead of the usual appeal for funds, a promissory note signed by Luisa for the sum of two hundred thousand dollars to be paid as soon as the Hatfield estate is settled and she had access to that much money."

"Luisa! I wouldn't put it past her to get rid of anyone who got in her way," Tommy said, "and what a motive that gives her! But if you'll tell me how she could get out of that apartment of hers, where there must be at least half a dozen servants, and down an elevator where everyone knows her, I'll buy it."

"You're familiar with the apartment?" Clark asked casually.

"Of course I'm familiar with it. I've known Fillmore for more than ten years, and I've been there at least half a dozen times."

"She could manage that," I said confidently. "The day she came here you wouldn't have known her, with dead-white makeup and a blond wig and cheap, ill-fitting clothes. Summers asked if she'd gone down the freight elevator. It must have been something like that. At least it could have been something like that and anyone could get into Summers's apartment unnoticed."

"With a passkey."

"I'll bet Luisa had a key."

Clark was amused by my obvious desire to convict Luisa.

"It could have been like that," he conceded.

"And what," Tommy demanded, "did the police make of that promissory note? Have they followed up Luisa yet?"

"So far," Clark admitted, "I haven't taken the police into my confidence."

I felt my heart sink. Allan had suggested that Clark was in search of a quick buck. With this as a hold over Luisa—No, I refused to believe it.

"My God," Tommy exploded, "here you are, throwing dirty looks at me because I have no alibi for last night, and implying that Kate could be implicated in this filthy mess, while you hold the whole key to the situation in your hand. What are you waiting for, Clark? A rake-off from Luisa?"

As he lunged forward, Clark held him off with one big hand against his chest. "Don't make a fool of yourself, Tommy. I could break you in two if I wanted to. Which, incidentally, I don't. But I'd like to sit on this for another twenty-four hours."

"Why?"

"Breaking someone's nerve."

"Someone?" The two men looked at each other for a long moment.

"Well, we have two murders now. I suppose there's not the same hesitation about committing a third. Whether Luisa killed Summers or not, we have her sweating it out, wondering what happened to that promissory note and when it will show up. And we must not forget Mike."

"Oh," I said, as though I'd been punched.

"I want him alive," Clark said.

"And what do you expect to happen in twenty-four hours to change the picture?" Tommy asked.

"Almost anything."

Tommy drew so deeply on his cigarette that he burned his lip.

"Almost anything. Nerves are being rasped. The situation has got out of control. Nothing has worked out according to the original sketch. And when that happens, people panic."

Tommy's expression changed. "You think you see it, don't you?"

"Well, I had a theory, which is a bit shaken now, but I'm still willing to gamble on it."

"Gamble with Kate?"

Again that long exchange of looks. Clark turned to me, his face sober. "Kate?"

"If it would bring Mike back," I said, "gamble with me."

"Good girl. Hold tight and don't let Luisa lure you out again. Or anyone else. I'll be busy. You look out for yourself, youngster."

Clark touched Tommy's arm. "Dr. Dixon prescribes a shave, a shower, and a change of clothes, followed by a decent meal. Strictly temperance. Be seeing you."

For a moment Tommy stood prodding at the burned-out cigarette in the ash tray and then he turned abruptly and I heard him go up the stairs to his apartment. He walked slowly as though he were spent.

Fourteen

When Tommy finally came down to the office, he was freshly shaven and cleaned up, but all his jauntiness was gone and there was no laughter in his eyes. For a moment I thought he was going to walk past me and then he stopped, looked down at me, and touched with a gentle finger the cheek that Summers had struck, tracing the mark of the bruises his hand had left.

As though a fire had been lighted, he kissed me, and I was on fire too, experiencing such rapture as I had never even suspected.

Whether it was a minute or an eternity, I did not know. And then Tommy thrust me away from him roughly.

"This won't do."

Still in the sway of that mood, I asked vaguely, "What won't?"

He gave me a little shake. "You—and me. It won't work, Kate. You're too young for me. I've been around. A lot. And that's the way I like it."

I was still bemused. "Whatever you like, Tommy."

182

"No," he groaned. "You're a nice girl, Kate. A pretty girl. A sweet girl. But you're not for me and I'm not for you." When I did not move or speak, he said, with that new impatience, "What are you waiting for, Kate? For heaven's sake, marry Allan and get out of this mess. Keep away from me. I'm bad medicine for a girl like you. Even Clark, who's an old friend, doesn't trust me farther than he can throw me."

"What makes you think so?"

"Because Summers isn't the only one with a tail. I have an escort wherever I go."

"One of Clark's men?"

"Nice, isn't it? Or perhaps it's the police. That would be even nicer." He went to open the door for me. "Downstairs, youngster. And stay there until your Allan can take care of you. He'll do a good job, you know. A lot better than I ever could."

Without a word I went past him, down to the basement, where I sat staring at the wall, not really unhappy. I was too numb for that. And then I roused myself to switch on the television set. For the first time in my life the news impinged on my own life because I was involved in the Hatfield murder and I had to know what was coming next. My future as well as Mike's was entangled with the whole affair.

It was too early for a news program on the television, so I got out Mike's little transistor radio. Dan Summers's murder was public now and linked, inevitably, to the killing of Fillmore Hatfield. The aging actress's story was given full play: the knock-down-and-drag-out fight, the later arrival of a drunk who pounded on the door and demanded admittance, the escape of a redheaded girl, not more than sixteen, and cute, if you liked them small—the actress herself was built along more Junoesque lines. And finally, late at night, the sound of a shot.

The police were noncommittal, except that they agreed it was too much of a coincidence for Mr. Hatfield and his chief assistant to be murdered within a few days of each other, unless there was some link between the crimes. Attempts were being made to learn the identity of the man who had given Summers a beating, as this indicated a person prone to the same kind of violence responsible for Hatfield's hideous beating. And particularly they wanted to know the identity of the redheaded girl.

The news commentator switched to a warm discussion between two men as to the country's pressing need for another sports stadium, and I turned it off. At a time of world upheaval it seemed to me that the last thing we needed was a place in which men could play games. While world leadership was slipping from our hands, we were settling for circuses.

I had never before sat idly in the little apartment. Weekdays I was in the agency until five. Weekends I scurried around doing chores and shopping and planning meals and taking care of the laundry and cleaning up. All the usual things. But this afternoon I just sat, feeling dull, feeling heavy, feeling numb.

Allan knocked twice before I could arouse myself enough to go to the door. He had looked in the agency, but Tommy had said I'd quit for the day, or just quit, it hadn't been clear.

"Quit," I said.

"Oh, good!" Allan lifted me off my feet and swung me around. "What are we waiting for? You should see the orders I got lined up! We'll be in the Big Time before you know it."

He flicked the tiny diamond on my finger. "We'll throw that away and get a real one."

I covered it protectingly with my hand. "We won't do any such thing. I don't want diamonds. Just peace. And rest. And safety."

"Then," he said, "let's start now."

"Start where?"

"We'll go see my doctor up on Eighty-fourth Street, and get our blood tests. Monday we'll get our license. And then you'll move into my apartment and transform it into a home, Kate darling. And in a few months, perhaps before the end of the year, we'll move to a better address. I'll be able to afford it by then. After all, I'm going to get something out of this deal."

And we did. As a kind of omen the sun, which had been hiding behind clouds all day, came bursting out, turning the steel and glass buildings into dazzling light. We drove through Central Park in a musty old taxicab, its floor cluttered with cigarette butts, but outside there were flowering bushes and the pale green of new buds and children buying balloons and popcorn. Mercifully the driver was not one of those garrulous men who have to unburden their souls to each passenger, so we made the ride in silence, holding hands.

I spoke only once, seeing Allan clearly with the sun on his face. "You look so tired!"

He smiled. "Just a weary old man? You'll be surprised," and his hand tightened on mine.

Allan's physician, whom he had chosen simply because he lived nearby, had a shabby waiting room where only a couple of patients looked over old magazines. When Allan's turn came, the nurse took us into the consulting room. To my surprise, the doctor was very young.

He saw my surprise and grinned like a conspiratorial schoolboy. "I have my proper diplomas," he assured me gravely. "The general rack and ruin around me is not a sign of decrepitude. It's a sign of getting started. I took over the practice of an old guy who had given up. Give me a year and I'll be on Park Avenue."

"And head of a major hospital," I agreed solemnly.

The doctor seemed to be pleased when Allan explained that we had come for blood tests. "Marriage is the right idea. Every now and then I've nearly committed matrimony myself. There's nothing like a first mortgage to settle a man down."

"Wait until you have to slap on a second mortgage," Allan told him.

"Hey," the young doctor said, "this guy is a pessimist. You could do better, lady. How about me?"

"Another word like that," I said severely, "and I'll sue you for malpractice."

It wasn't until we had left the doctor's office and Allan was about to hail a cab, that I stopped him. "We can't afford all these cabs. A bus will do just as well."

He laughed but did not protest when I turned toward the bus stop. "Just like your mother. God, I'm a lucky man. You know I've had some bad moments, thinking maybe you and Tommy—"

"Oh, no," I said lightly, "not at all. I'm not Tommy's type, you know," but some of the sunshine had gone out of the day.

186

"I didn't know he limited himself to a single type," Allan commented dryly.

That was when I noticed the man who had been standing beside a mailbox, apparently reading the schedule of mail pickups, and who was now sauntering in our direction. I had seen him staring down the alley when we had come out of the basement, though I had not been aware of noticing him at the time. So many people made a habit of stopping to look at the alley where Fillmore Hatfield's body had been found, as though they expected to find some tangible evidence of the murder.

I clutched Allan's arm and leaned close to him, keeping my voice low. Seeing my unaccustomed gesture, Allan smiled tenderly and his hand closed over mine.

"I'm being followed," I told him. "A man in jeans and a windbreaker. His hair is dark brown and sort of long."

"Your eyes are as big as an owl's," Allan told me. "What makes you think you are being followed?"

"Because I saw him when we left the apartment. He was just standing there, staring down the alley. It can't be coincidence, Allan, his turning up here."

The smile faded. Allan half turned. "I'll have a word with him."

"No, don't. I think it may be someone working for Clark Dixon."

"And why is he having you followed?"

"Just to make sure I'm safe, I suppose. That would be like him. And now that description of me is on the radio—did you hear it?—the red-haired girl who ran away from Summers and who might have gone back in the night to kill him,

187

I guess Clark wants to keep an eye on me."

"I think I can manage to do that myself," Allan said. "You're going to be my wife in a few days, Kate. I'll have the right I've wanted since the first day I saw you to look after you. What I'd like—" He broke off.

"What's that, Allan?"

"To give you Mike as a wedding present."

"I wish you could." But there was no real hope in my voice. Not any more. Mike with his rough thatch of red hair and his lopsided smile seemed to be going farther away all the time.

"You don't really have much faith in my abilities, do you, darling? Perhaps the old man will manage to pass a miracle yet." But his mind was only half on what he was saying. He was listening, as I was listening, to the following footsteps.

When the bus pulled in at the curb, I got on and found a seat at the window while Allan was counting out exact change. In New York you pay exact change or you walk. So I had a chance to see the man who followed him into the bus. When Allan joined me, he looked casually at the man who went past us without a single glance and took a seat halfway down the bus, just behind the center door, so he'd have a quick exit if necessary.

"There's just one thing I hope," I whispered to Allan, who bent near me to hear, "and that is that Luisa is being followed too."

"Luisa!"

I told him about the promissory note that Dan Summers had hidden, in which Luisa agreed to pay him $200,000 as soon as the Hatfield estate was settled. "And that," I added, "is one reason why I think she killed Summers."

"Quiet," he said in a low tone. "Be careful! You mustn't say things like that. You've got to curb that unruly tongue of yours or you'll get in trouble I can't get you out of."

"Bet you could," I said, and I laughed.

II

Saturday morning. Still no response to the big ad in the newspapers reading:

Will the individual who mailed a dog whistle on a metal tag to Joe Blanchard Monday in New York please call the following number or apply in person at the address below. Reward.

Perhaps no one had mailed it; perhaps the one who had did not read the ads; I didn't read them myself. Perhaps he or she had left the city or forgotten the incident. Or perhaps Mike himself had done it, his only way of sending out a message about his whereabouts, as he was unlikely to have paper and pencil with him, and, by the end of the week, he certainly could have had nothing left of his allowance. I was fairly sure most of it had gone into the purchase of the dog whistle.

On Saturday mornings the television is directed chiefly at children—not very bright children. There was nothing new on the Dan Summers murder on the radio. Mrs. Hatfield had issued a statement indicating her shock at hearing of the wanton murder of her husband's trusted friend and associate of some years. It seemed to her that a wave of terror was breaking over Manhattan, at least over the Hatfield world.

When I had finished breakfast, I sat turning around and

around on my finger Allan's ring, trying to make myself realize that in a few days I would be married. I would be Allan's wife. The future would be different. A new life.

When I had done the few dishes and changed my bed, I went into Mike's room. The bed there didn't need changing. I had done it a week ago and it had not been slept in since. I opened the window to air the room, looked out, trying to imagine the scene that had met his eyes while he was preparing for Joe's birthday party, fingering the dog whistle for which I suspected that he had deprived himself for a week of chocolate bars.

I pushed aside the curtain that concealed his meager wardrobe and looked at the familiar, shabby garments, the scuffed shoes. It was bathos and I knew it. I knew too that Mike, if he were to see me sniffling like this over a pair of patched shoes, would laugh at me. Or would he laugh again? I thrust the thought away from me fiercely, for though I did not hope much, still I hoped.

Clark's sturdy knock made me pull myself together and blow my nose before I went to admit him. He stood looming up in the doorway, almost filling it, his head ducked a little so he could get in without knocking it on the lintel, taking in with one swift glance the marks of tears.

"There's no answer to the ad," I said uselessly, because, of course, he knew that.

"Early days yet," he said cheerfully.

There was no point in commenting on that. I said instead, "Thank you, Clark, for having your man keep an eye on me. But, honestly, I don't think it is necessary and it must be awfully expensive."

There was a moment's silence and then Clark said easily,

"Don't give it a thought. And so far his duties haven't been very onerous. I understand you and your Allan paid a call on a doctor yesterday. Blood tests?"

I nodded.

"Kind of a rush, isn't it?"

I nodded again. "But that's what Allan wants, and anyhow I can't go on staying here, and Tommy—doesn't need me in the agency any longer, so it seems to be the most sensible move. Don't you think so?"

"I'm fresh out of advice today," Clark said. "Anyhow, I've never set up as Advice to the Lovelorn." He stood hovering over me. "What are your plans?"

"About getting married?"

"No, about today."

"Well, I haven't any. Just waiting."

"Then I have an idea. Why don't you come along with me? My guy's off today, so how about being looked after by the head of the firm himself?"

"But there can't be any danger for me, Clark, now that Summers is dead."

"Of course not. But a guy gets lonely. Come on," he added cajolingly.

"Where are we going?"

"I've got a kind of idea working around in my head. There's one person I'd like very much to talk to—Luisa's theatrical agent. He must know as much about her as anyone. I have a kind of hunch. Coming?"

"If there's a chance of digging up something against Luisa, you couldn't keep me away," I assured him.

He grinned. "You're a little wildcat, and you look like a nice, fluffy kitten. All right, pull in those claws, get your coat and we're on our way."

He drove a battered yellow Volkswagen that sounded like a collection of loose bolts and into which he folded himself up like a jackknife. Luisa's theatrical agent occupied a couple of rooms on Forty-fourth Street. A man was standing near the curb, reading a newspaper, as Clark and I left the car and walked along looking for the number. Clark paused to ask him for a match, thanked him, and joined me, a lighted cigarette in his hand.

"Very smooth," I said.

Clark grinned. "You're getting too bright for your own good."

"Well, you had a full strip of matches. Who is he following?"

"Luisa."

"You mean you think she's with her agent?"

"I devoutly hope so. Apparently my idea is paying off."

We went up a narrow staircase between two theaters, and into a dingy waiting room where a haggard woman, whose hair had been dyed so often that it was of no determinate shade, sat reading a play script in a bored manner and ignoring a boy with long hair and a long but scanty beard who sat on an unupholstered settee reading *Variety*. A woman came up the stairs behind us, a woman who looked vaguely familiar until I heard her voice and then I recognized her at once from having seen her in character parts in a number of movies.

"Hi, Wendy. Anything stirring?"

The receptionist looked up. "Hi, Marcia. Nothing today. It's a tough season for casting, you know, particularly in the spring."

"You're telling me!"

"Biddy Blanchard has been prowling around, trying to get some financing for a new show her troupe is putting on. I don't know whether she's casting yet. You might give her a buzz."

"Here today and gone tomorrow," the actress said in disillusionment.

"Not with Biddy's shows. They don't pay top salaries, but they have prestige value—" As the actress made a derisive sound, Wendy added, "And she's got a faithful clientele. Subscription seats, and the list keeps growing. Her shows run longer and longer. Last one ran for a year and a half and may come to Broadway yet."

"Well, it's always worth a try. Be seeing you." The actress turned away, turned back. "Anyhow, thanks for the tip."

The receptionist, with the unlikely name of Wendy, which seemed perennially youthful, looked from me to Clark, her eyes resting approvingly on his big frame. I'll say for Clark that, unlike the late and unlamented Summers, he was not conscious of his attraction for women, at least he didn't play on it.

"We'd like to see Mr. Weinberg."

"Looking for a job? You can leave your pictures, if you like, and a résumé of your experience. But there's nothing doing right now unless you want summer stock." Like most New Yorkers, she regarded summer stock as tantamount to deportation.

"This is a personal matter. He won't know our names. And we won't take up much of his time."

"Well, you can't," Wendy said, "because he's not here."

The boy looked up at that. "Why," he asked indignantly,

"didn't you tell me that?"

"Oh, he'll be back. I did tell you it isn't any use waiting. Mr. Weinberg is taking off a month and not adding any new clients in the meantime. On your way, kid. You're wasting your time and mine."

The boy went out, walking with a disciplined grace that surprised me. Apparently he was not a hopeful beginner but a professional.

"When do you expect Mr. Weinberg?" Clark asked.

Wendy looked at her watch and put the play she was reading in a briefcase. "I don't know. He said twelve-thirty, but he's probably in a bar on Ninth Avenue right now and may not get back for hours."

"May we wait?"

She hesitated. Then she shrugged. "Why not? There's nothing to steal, God knows. There's already someone waiting in his office. Hope dies hard in some people, though I knew she didn't have a chance. I'm clearing out for the day. But, like a housewife, my work is never done." She patted the briefcase, pulled on a rakish-looking coat and went out.

When her heavy steps had gone down the stairs Clark, moving like a cat, went to ease open the door of the inner office. There was no mistaking Luisa's voice, and I nodded vigorously at Clark's inquiring look.

"We've got to talk . . . There's something of Dan's you've got to get for me . . . It's absolutely essential . . . I have a key to the apartment and no cracks from you."

I realized then that she was alone, talking over the telephone. She made this clear herself. "Of course I'm not fool enough to be talking from home. I don't think the phone is tapped, but there are half a dozen extensions and I'm not

194

taking any chances. At least, no chance I don't have to take. I'm at my agent's and he's not here. . . . No one would know me, looking like this. . . . I don't care how you do it, but we're walking in quicksand right now and we've got to get out. . . . We both made mistakes, bad mistakes. I'm not denying that. What we've got to do is patch things up, cover up . . ."

Her voice rose almost hysterically. "You've got to find it. You've got to. . . . You're damned right it will be worth your while . . . a promissory note to Dan for two hundred thousand dollars. Find it and I'll give you the same. You'd never see that much in any other way in your whole life. . . . Nonsense, you're the only man . . . But there's something else. I don't like having a witness around. It's like a time bomb ready to go off . . . I don't believe it. There's only one way to handle it. Get rid of the kid . . . I know you couldn't help him stumbling on it, but it has to be done. And that goes for the girl too . . . I tell you she's dangerous. She's the kind who won't give up. . . . You'd better meet me at the place on Fifty-seventh Street. No one will notice me. You'd better get there!" She banged down the telephone and Clark eased the door closed and drew me down the stairs.

"Clark!" I protested.

"Wait until we can mix with the crowd on the street," he warned me, looked for the loitering man who was now studying a playbill, nodded briefly and steered me onto the sidewalk, across the street at the corner and leaned against the side of a building, looking toward the narrow staircase to the agent's office. A moment later a woman came out—a woman with a dead-white face and a blond wig, wearing a shabby coat that was too big and too long for her.

I grabbed Clark's arm. He stared unbelievingly, even when his man turned to drop in behind her without looking in her direction. "That's Luisa?"

"That's Luisa. That's the way she looked when she came to the agency to see Tommy. Clark, we know everything now, don't we?" I was sick at heart.

"Everything," he said, "except where Mike is."

Fifteen

"Are you just going to let her go, Clark?" I stared at him unbelievingly.

He made one of his rare gestures, for he was a quiet man. "What do you think I could accomplish, Kate?"

"You aren't even going to talk to her?"

"Perhaps you'd like me to say: 'Did you murder Dan Summers to retrieve that promissory note? Did you plan your husband's murder? Did you,'" for a moment Clark hesitated and then he went on steadily, "'did you incite your accomplice to murder Mike—and Kate?' Can you imagine Luisa breaking down and pouring out a confession?"

"And knowing what she—what they intend to do to Mike and me, you're just standing there?"

"They also serve," he began and saw my expression. "That's a good man I have following Luisa. He won't lose her."

"He must have slipped up when she killed Summers."

"He wasn't primed about the disguise and the delivery elevator at the Hatfield building then. And we have to say,

197

if she killed him. Oh, I agree that it is the most likely solution. But right now we can't do anything without evidence. Luisa is going to have to make a move, and this time there will be no slip-up. When she does, we'll be there, complete with a policeman equipped with bracelets."

"Do you have a man following Tommy, too?"

"Of course."

"And who is going to pay for all this?"

"Oh, the Lord will provide," Clark said easily and I could have choked him. Well, no, I couldn't, but I'd have liked to.

"Why don't you tell me the truth, Clark? It was never Hatfield who was the center of all this; it is Luisa."

"It's Luisa," he admitted. "She sparked the whole deal and she couldn't have carried it out alone. But now the scenario has been changed. There have been too many fatal factors. First, Mike, for the first time since you moved to that basement apartment, was at home and looking out of the window at the moment when Hatfield was killed. Then there was a promise of marriage Luisa never intended to keep and, in any case, because of Hatfield's foresight, doesn't want to keep; then there was a promissory note in payment of blackmail, which Luisa intended to retrieve. And failed. And now Luisa is desperate. She is terrified for fear that note will turn up sooner or later, and whenever it does, she will be in the worst trouble she has ever known. Right now she has to move, or get her accomplice to move for her, and that is where we step in."

"And save Mike?"

"If we possibly can, Kate. I can't promise more than that."

"How good are the chances?"

"Fifty-fifty."

198

"What do we do now?"

"If you aren't tied up with Allan, why don't you lunch with me?"

"No, I haven't a date with Allan, but it's early. Would you like to go with me to his display room? I've never seen it."

"Fine, let's go."

As he turned, looking for a cab, I said, "It's not far. Let's walk."

Already heavy coats were disappearing, replaced by lighter and brighter clothes. Store windows were displaying Easter hats and dresses. The windows of a florist's shop were filled with lilies.

"One of the first things I heard when I came to New York," I told Clark, "was about the woman who entered a Madison Avenue florist's shop and wanted to buy carnations. The clerk looked down his nose and said, "Madam, this is not a carnation neighborhood.""

"That's carriage trade for you, the kind to which you'd like to be accustomed."

"Not me. I don't like orchids. I'd rather have roses any day," and I remembered Allan telling me that red tulips were my flowers.

"Just a shade common perhaps," Clark said gravely, and I made a face at him. One thing about Clark, big and stable and in full control, he would not allow you to remain tense or worried. There was a kind of large sanity about him.

The Madison Avenue building was between Fifty-sixth and Fifty-seventh Streets, an ideal place for an art display. In the lobby we searched the directory. Drummond's Ceramics was domiciled in room 909. When we got out of the elevator, we had to wander around to find the right number.

A man was just coming out as we arrived and he paused, looking at us.

"Were you coming here?"

"Are we too late?" Clark asked.

"Well, I was closing up, but there's no hurry. We're always glad to have people drop in." He acted as though it did not happen very often.

I was surprised that Clark did not say he knew Allan or that I was Allan's fiancée, but I assumed he knew what he was doing.

Fillmore Hatfield's big opportunity for Allan to display his wares on Madison Avenue was one small room on a dark court. There were three long tables holding ceramics and at the back a desk where orders could be made out, a cash box fitted into a desk drawer, indicating that not much money exchanged hands, and a telephone. Well-lighted corner cupboards held a few special pieces, among which I found the one of my mother, the laughing man, the old man reading, and the nun.

There were, of course, a number of pieces that I had never seen before, many of them the standard commercial kind of thing, a few that were really good, revealing all Allan's sharp wit and keen observation.

The salesman hovered over us like an anxious hen, picking up one piece after another to display its particular qualities.

"Mr. Drummond is a real artist," he told us earnestly. "He is making an art form out of a medium that for too long has been chiefly commercial." He looked hopefully at Clark. "Did you have anything particular in mind, sir?"

"No, but I was naturally interested," Clark said, and the

salesman nodded as though he knew what he was talking about.

I turned to Clark. "Allan did a marvelous one of Luisa, which Mr. Hatfield commissioned, but I can't find it here."

"You know Mr. Drummond?" the clerk asked.

Clark cut in before I could be indiscreet, as he was, to his cost, beginning to know me and my undisciplined tongue. "Where did you see that?"

"In his apartment. That's how he happened to meet her. Mr. Hatfield commissioned it."

"Oh, the portrait of Mrs. Hatfield. Well, now, that's a pity, it really is, but as I said, Mr. Drummond is a true artist, not commercial at all. After Mr. Hatfield's tragic death, he felt that it would be an act of disrespect for the dead, and indeed for his widow, to put portraits of her on sale. They would be bought by vulgar curiosity seekers, you know, and that's not at all the clientele Mr. Drummond wants to attract. So he had the mold and all the copies destroyed. A great pity in a way, but one can only respect the motive behind it. No money sense. But artists haven't, of course." The clerk's hand flapped on a limp wrist.

"Thanks a lot for your time," Clark said.

"It doesn't matter. I was just going to close up for the day. Not much business on Saturdays, you know."

"Not much business any time," Clark remarked when we were on the street again.

"But Allan got some big orders this week. He was exultant about it. He swears he'll be in the Big Time in a year and making lots of money."

"So then you promptly fell into his arms," Clark jeered at me.

"What I can't understand, Clark, is why someone hasn't taken a poke at you."

"I'm too big," he said simply, and I had to laugh. "You know, Kate," he said seriously, "your Allan has real talent. Some of his work is enchanting. Damn it, it ought to sell. But I wish I could have seen the one of Luisa. I'd like to know what that artist's eye of his made of her."

"There's a copy in his apartment."

"Let's go ask to see it and then we can all three go out to lunch."

"He'll be busy all day in Red Bank filling orders."

"Well, you have a nice honest face, though I can't say much more for it." Clark pretended to duck. "Let's go try your feminine wiles and talk our way in."

I agreed.

"What did you make of it?"

I hesitated. "Well, she's beautiful, of course, with big hungry eyes and a greedy mouth. He caught the salient things, but I think he missed the hardness; perhaps because he saw only the—the hunger."

"Or the greed?" Clark suggested.

I shook my head. "I don't think so."

Whether it was my feminine wiles or the ten-dollar bill Clark gave him, the superintendent admitted us to Allan's apartment without question. I went at once to the table where my portrait had stood with the three contrasting women surrounding it. There was nothing now but the cabinet portrait of me, which Allan had taken from the Red Bank house without permission, when he was helping us to move.

202

And behind it was a tall vase of red tulips.

All of a sudden I was ashamed that we were in Allan's apartment in his absence, ashamed that I had seen this token of his devotion. I felt that I had been spying on him.

"It isn't here any more," I said. "All the ceramic portraits he had are gone."

"So I notice."

"Let's go, Clark."

"Just a minute. I'd like to call my answering service. There may be some messages and I've been out of touch all morning. Okay?"

I sat down on the one comfortable chair to wait, picked up my handkerchief and tucked it in my coat pocket, and listened while Clark dialed, identified himself, and then listened. Whatever he heard upset him. "So that's it! And I kept hoping I was wrong." He put down the telephone, said, "Look here, Kate, I've got to leave you. Take care of yourself. And remember—it won't be long now."

There hadn't been time for lunch and I was starving. It was early for dinner, but I got off the bus when I saw a brightly lighted cafeteria and went in. When I had finished my early supper or late lunch—New Yorkers eat at all hours —I decided to walk home. I was in no hurry to return to that silence, that waiting. *It won't be long now.* It had better not be. Because Luisa had sent out her orders that Mike was to die.

Lights were already beginning to appear in the opal dusk when I reached the Village and walked down a street hushed with late Saturday afternoon quiet. I fumbled for the key before I went down to the basement. Perhaps because I was on edge and ready to start at shadows, I felt that someone was behind me, aware of a swift movement, and I ducked. Something struck me and I pitched forward on my face.

When I opened my eyes, I was lying on the couch in the living room. I groped at my forehead. My fingers were sticky with blood and Tommy was bending over me. It would have been easier to die, I thought then.

"Don't try to move," he said. "I don't think you've broken anything. At least nothing felt broken." He went into the kitchen and came back with a bowl of warm water and began to bathe my forehead gently. Before my fascinated eyes the water turned pink, but Tommy reassured me. "Just a gash. It bled quite a bit, but I'm sure that's all."

"If it was yours," I said indignantly, "you wouldn't be so complacent."

"I know it must hurt like the devil, but really you're all right. If you like, I'll call Dad's doctor. He seems to be a good guy."

"What happened to me?"

"You stumbled and fell down the steps and knocked yourself out."

Knocked myself out! I tried to remember the vague impression I had had. Just nerves. It could have been true.

"Where were you?"

"I was worried about you, out on your own, and God knows what might be happening to you."

"There weren't any lights in here."

He gave me an odd look. "I fell asleep," he admitted. "I haven't had much sleep lately."

I tried to straighten out my thoughts, what I knew, what I thought I knew, what I suspected—and feared.

"Tommy," and I held out my hand, "give me your key to

this place, will you?"

He handed it to me without a word and left the apartment. I saw his legs pass the window.

After a few moments I tried in a gingerly fashion to get off the couch and found, after a moment of dizziness, that I was all right, though I had rubbery legs. I picked up the bowl to empty it and the handkerchief with which Tommy had bathed my forehead. It was a lacy affair I had never seen before and in one corner was embroidered a big fancy L.

And after a long time I dialed Clark's number and told him of what had happened. He said nothing but, "I see. Yes, I see. Okay, leave it to me, Kate. You'll be all right."

"*I'll* be all right. What about Mike?"

"Haven't you guessed yet where he is, Kate?" Without waiting for my reply, he broke the connection.

I sat on in the dark for some time until I heard the familiar rattle of the yellow Volkswagen and then long legs passed my window without stopping, and Clark ran up the steps to the agency.

That night I took two sleeping pills and fell asleep as though I had been slugged as, come to think of it, I had. I dreamed of Mike in the new green sweater and woke up with my pillow wet with tears.

Sixteen

Sunday morning. There was a lump on my forehead where I had fallen—or been pushed down the stairs. It hurt like blazes but not as much as the sick knowledge I carried in my heart.

"Are you sure you wouldn't rather come and stay with us?" Biddy Blanchard asked over the telephone. "We'd love to have you and there are two extra bedrooms. No trouble at all. It would be better than just waiting."

"I'll be all right," I told her. "And I won't be here long. Allan Drummond and I are planning to take out our wedding license."

"I'm so glad for you and so relieved. I hated having you alone in that basement, just waiting."

The ad was still running in the Sunday papers but there had been no response. By now it was unlikely that anyone would answer it. The Hatfield case was still on the front page because of the Summers murder and the disappearance of the redheaded girl. Television, in fact, was having a fine time with the redheaded girl, trying to link her with the Hatfield murder. As Luisa was so hell-bent on getting rid of me, I wondered that she did not put in an anonymous call to the police, identifying me. But, of course, she knew that I would talk then.

There was the usual war news from a world said to be at peace, the usual brief accounts of bizarre happenings around New York. An out-of-work man had found a metal box containing $40,000 in small bills and turned it in to the police. The generous owner gave him a $5 reward. A cab driver had pulled up at the precinct with a dead woman in his cab. She had been all right when he picked her up outside a cafeteria and asked him to take her to Grand Central. When she failed to get out of the cab, he found her dead, and had assumed a heart attack. Examination revealed that she had been poisoned. So far no identification had been made.

I wandered aimlessly around the apartment and then, remembering that my wedding day was almost upon me and I had made no preparations at all, I got out my clothes, stacked them on my bed, and began to go through them, separating the things that needed to be dry-cleaned and mended. But I found I wasn't getting anything accomplished. I was standing in the middle of the room, holding a wool skirt in my hands, staring into space.

This wouldn't do. I was putting off what had to be done. Moving quickly before I could change my mind, I went to the telephone and called Clark.

He answered so promptly that I thought he must have been waiting for a call.

"Clark, I want to go to the police and tell them every single thing I know. I can't take any more chances on Mike. I've waited more than a week without any result. Now I've got to play it the other way. I don't know where he is; I have no way of finding out by myself. I can't afford to wait any longer."

I could almost feel Clark thinking. "What about Tommy?" he asked at length.

"What else can I do, Clark? I'm the only one Mike has, and last night he nearly lost me. I didn't lose my balance and stumble. Someone aimed at the back of my head and I ducked. Someone thought he had killed me. Mike's the only one I have any right to think of now. You see that, don't you?"

I was aware of the anguish in my voice so I was surprised by the cheerfulness with which Clark said, "You're quite right, Kate. I'll pick you up in about twenty minutes."

There were only a few men in the dingy precinct room when we went in. Clark asked to see Lieutenant Carfare and after a few minutes we went behind a counter and into a smaller room which held a battered desk, a few uncomfortable chairs, several phones, a huge ash tray filled with cigarette butts, and two men. The older one, Lieutenant Carfare, was sitting behind the desk, looking through a file; the other, named Forman, was young, pleasant, and trim in his uniform. Both men stood up and Lieutenant Carfare grinned at Clark.

"Well, what have you come to confess, Dixon? Murder, rape, bank robbery?"

"All three," Clark answered as they shook hands. He introduced me. "Katherine Forbes, Lieutenant Carfare, whom I met in the service and who got me all involved in crime. And if you tell him your story about the encyclopedia, he'll slap you in chains and throw you in a dungeon."

208

The lieutenant nodded. "That's the standard procedure."
I gathered by all this lighthearted persiflage that they were
old friends so, I felt, if not happier, at least more confident.

"Now, Kate," Clark said, "it's your story."

"Just a minute," intervened the lieutenant, "you've
aroused my curiosity. What is this encyclopedia story?"

"Under intelligence," I explained, "in the index, that is,
there are three headings: intelligence, human; intelligence,
animal; intelligence, military."

"The dungeon it is. Now then—" He sat back and the
younger man, giving me a friendly smile, opened a notebook.
It was about as frightening as a kaffeeklatsch.

I took a long breath and then told them every single thing
I knew. I began with Mike's excited call to Joe and his
disappearance, my attempts to interest the Missing Persons
Bureau, the threatening call, and then the later call that
claimed to be from Rochester saying Mike was fine; and then
the dog whistle which had been mailed in New York on
Monday and made nonsense of the Rochester call. So that
one must have been made under duress. There was no doubt
about it being Mike. Allan knew him too well to be deceived.

The lieutenant, smoking and relaxed, paused for a moment
to send the young policeman out for coffee for us all and then
nodded. "Go on, Miss Forbes."

I'd come to the dangerous part now, the arrival of Fillmore Hatfield in the agency the day he was murdered in the
alley next door. I half expected a hand to descend on my
shoulder and drag me off to a cell for having withheld perti-
nent information, but the lieutenant nodded, not appearing
to be at all surprised, and said only, "Go on. Don't hurry,
Miss Forbes. We want everything you can give us."

So I told him that Hatfield had asked for Tommy and that he had been prepared to meet him as an enemy and how he had finally believed my statement that Tommy was not in New York. So then Hatfield had said he might as well get some value out of his visit and wanted Mr. Eakins to arrange for a secret honeymoon trip because he had to get out of the city at once. His life had been threatened.

"So he must have been killed just after he left the agency," I said. And then the coffee tasted vile and I pushed it aside, knowing with I had done to Tommy.

"Go on," the lieutenant said again, and Clark gave me his encouraging smile, but then he wasn't involved. It didn't matter to him except as a case to be solved.

So I went on to say that on the day before Hatfield died, Dan Summers had come to the office, demanding to see Tommy and swearing that he had seen him in a Village night club with the girl who had since married Hatfield. He had informed Hatfield, who, in retaliation, had inserted a news item in the papers indicating that the Eakins Travel Agency was bankrupt. He had established the agency some time before as what he himself referred to as a "private charity."

"Go on," the lieutenant said.

I went on to Luisa's appearance in the office, disguised and calling herself Mrs. Stevenson; her meeting with Dan Summers who, as I realized later, was blackmailing her as well as baiting her. Later, Luisa had telephoned me and asked, or rather ordered me to come and see her, when I let her know I was aware of her identity. She said if I didn't go I'd never see Mike again.

I described the visit and how, on leaving, I had been forced by Summers, who was waiting on the street, to go to his hotel where he threatened to do away with me unless I could persuade Tommy to sign a confession that he had killed Hatfield. He promised that he would never use it unless Tommy forced him to.

My mouth and throat were dry from talking and the young policeman went to get me a paper cup of water, which helped.

I went on to describe the arrival of the man who appeared to be drunk and who had made so much noise he forced Summers to open the door and how I had got away.

"Mercer," Clark intervened at this point and Carfare nodded.

"And that night Summers was shot to death and a woman described me as the one who had run away in the afternoon and probably had a motive for killing him. But I didn't, Lieutenant."

A smile twitched the corners of his mouth. "I'm sure you didn't, Miss Forbes."

"I think it was Luisa Hatfield who did it. She had the strongest motive." I thrust fiercely out of my mind the memory of Tommy's rage when he saw my cut lip and the beating he had administered to Summers. That didn't enter the picture.

"What makes you think Mrs. Hatfield is guilty?" the lieutenant asked.

"Tom—that is, we figured that she probably incited Summers to kill her husband and promised that she would marry him and he'd get a share in the money. But she never really meant to do it. Anyhow," I steadied my voice, "it was Tommy she wanted. Summers realized that when he found her at the agency."

Clark looked askance at Lieutenant Carfare and then pulled out of an inner pocket an envelope that he handed to the officer. It contained the promissory note.

There was an uncomfortable silence while the lieutenant read it, a more uncomfortable silence while he sat looking fixedly at Clark. "Getting too big for your britches, aren't you, Dixon? May I ask where you found this?"

Clark told him.

"And you thought it was okay to hold out on the police with a—a stick of dynamite like this?"

"Well, I had a kind of an idea—"

"You ought to lose your license for this." The lieutenant was doing a slow burn. "You know damned well you should never have taken it in the first place and you should have—"

"Okay," Clark said in his usual quiet manner, in marked contrast with the angry police officer. "I've had a bellyful of snooping, so take away my license. I'm ready to get out of the business. More than ready. I'm not making enough use of this big carcase of mine. I'm thinking of joining a group of guys who are working to preserve African wild life. It's dangerous and active and interesting. A more meaningful job than this one any day."

"I'm not so sure," the lieutenant said somberly,. "In the long run that may be the only kind of life we are able to save. Stay with it, Dixon. You got out of line this time but, hell, we need you more than any elephant does." He turned back to me. "Go on," he said.

"That's about all. Clark and I had heard Luisa order her accomplice to get rid of Mike and me and last night someone tried to kill me and I fell. But Tommy said I just stumbled

212

and knocked myself out." I went on to tell him the most damning thing of all. "And Tommy was bathing my head with Luisa's handkerchief." I held it out to him.

The lieutenant's eyes flickered toward Clark and back to the big ash tray. "What made you decide to come here today, Miss Forbes?"

"Mike. If anything happens to me there won't be anyone to find Mike. Can't you force Luisa to tell? Isn't there anything you can do?"

"I'm afraid not," the lieutenant said so emphatically that I sat staring at him in shocked disbelief.

"Nothing at all?"

"There's no way to make her speak, Miss Forbes. Luisa Hatfield is dead. She was found in a taxi late yesterday afternoon when her driver stopped at Grand Central. She had been poisoned. She was in disguise, a blond wig and dead-white make-up. There were no papers in her handbag. She wasn't identified until we got a report on her fingerprints. She'd been arrested a couple of times for lewd performances. Name of Luisa Bara."

He turned back to the file he had been reading when we came in. "The driver picked her up outside a cafeteria on Fifty-seventh Street. She was alone at the time. A cashier in the cafeteria remembers seeing her because of that chalk-white face. He thinks there was a man with her, wearing dark glasses, but he isn't sure and couldn't identify. All we know at this point is that she was given a quick-acting poison, probably in coffee. The doctors don't like to give out the names of poisons. Might give people ideas."

The catastrophe was so complete that I sat benumbed. Luisa was dead, the only person, except for her accomplice, who knew where Mike was hidden.

I realized that the lieutenant was still talking. "You are right in assuming that she probably murdered Dan Summers. Once we had her identification, we made a search of the Hatfield apartment. Boy, oh boy! I never knew before how one-tenth of one percent of the public lives. We found the murder gun hidden inside a shoe." He looked up at me for a moment. "We're looking for her accomplice, Miss Forbes. When she made that call from her agent's office, Summers was already dead. We're checking back now on all her boy friends, looking for someone deeply enough involved to help her out on a deal like this. Someone," he added thoughtfully, "who would do a lot to get quick money, if not for Luisa."

"The alluring Luisa," Clark murmured.

"Not when I saw her," the lieutenant said grimly. "Well, we're clearing up the names, one by one. The last man, before she married Hatfield, seems to have been Tommy Eakins." The lieutenant looked at me from under bushy brows that made him appear to be frowning even when he smiled. "But there are others. Unfortunately the lady only used initials in her diary. Very active life she appears to have led."

I had no comment to make. I'd told him every single thing I knew.

"We found a little ceramic figure, very clever, a portrait of her as she must have been. Work of a guy named Drummond, commissioned by Hatfield, who seems to have set him up in business. Another of his 'private charities,' I take it. And in a jewel box—wow! Di'monds, like the song says, are a girl's best friend."

"There's one point," Clark said. "Could she have killed

214

herself? We were closing in. She must have been scared out of her wits wondering about that promissory note. She was shaken by Summers's murder. Hatfield had tricked her so she couldn't collect on his millions until she was sixty. And Mike was still alive—Mike who would always be a menace. And suppose, just suppose, her accomplice refused to carry out her orders and get rid of Mike and Kate?"

"She would never have given up," I said. "Never in the world. She was a fighter like me." I pushed back my chair. "It's no use, is it, Clark? We might as well go."

"Sit down, Miss Forbes," Carfare said. "We have lots of time."

"But Mike hasn't. I'm going to look for him myself, if I have to search every inch of Manhattan."

"Why not leave it to us?"

"The Missing Persons Bureau? How much have they done? They never believed me. I doubt if they even tried to find him."

"I'm sorry about that. Actually we were given the impression that he was a lively, adventurous kid who made a habit of running away, or at least going off on his own. At least that's the impression given us by a family friend, Mr. Allan Drummond."

"Well, that's partly true except that he'd never stay away. Never. He's a responsible child." This time when I pushed back my chair the lieutenant made no attempt to stop me.

"Thank you for coming in and for your cooperation, Miss Forbes," he said politely, with no reference to the fact that I had deliberately withheld for a week vital information in the Hatfield killing. "But I'd like to make a suggestion. If I were you, I'd get out of that apartment for a day or so and go to a hotel where you'll be safe. And don't tell anyone except the police where you are going. Can you do that? If you can't afford it—"

"I can afford it if it's not too expensive. For one night, at least."

"That will probably be enough. The end is in sight, you know."

"The only thing is—"

"Well?"

"Suppose—just suppose Mike does come home and I'm not there. If I'm in danger, think how much worse—"

"Not to worry. We'll plant a man there from the time when you tell us that you are leaving."

Clark went home with me while I packed a suitcase. I realized then that he was taking on the job of watchdog. That was why he had accompanied me to the police, though it was obvious to me that he had already talked to them. I wondered how much he knew, how much the police knew, that I was not being told.

We didn't speak until we were nearly home. Then I said, "I don't see much point in bothering with a hotel. I've lost everything now, haven't I? Mike—and—" I did not go on.

The telephone was ringing when I unlocked the door, and I ran to answer it. The man at the other end of the wire said, "Are you the one who advertised about that dog whistle?"

"Yes! Oh, yes, I am!" At the excitement in my voice Clark, who had been about to light a cigarette, turned sharply in my direction. I nodded frantically at him.

"There isn't any trick about this, is there? I mean, what's so special about that whistle?"

"I think my little brother dropped it somewhere and he's

been abducted. He's been gone for over a week now, and he had that whistle with him when he disappeared."

"So that's it! Okay, my name is Brown Foster. I picked the thing up and carried it around in my pocket, forgot all about it until I was feeling for some tobacco on my way to work Monday morning. So then I saw the tag and I stamped and mailed it. I hope I haven't done any harm."

"Where did you find it?"

"I'm not exactly sure. Someplace near my house when I was taking a walk Saturday afternoon. I like to get what exercise I can over the weekends, you see."

"Where's home?"

"Oh, I see what you mean. I live in Red Bank, New Jersey."

Seventeen

Clark had taken the telephone out of my unresisting hand and was asking questions, getting the man's name, address, and telephone number. Now that he was convinced that he was not engaged in anything dangerous or illegal, the man seemed to be more than willing to cooperate. He assured Clark that he would be happy to testify if it should be necessary. Evidently the dog whistle had introduced him to more drama than he had ever known. He might even get his name in print.

Red Bank. That meant Allan! But it couldn't be Allan. And yet who else would have taken Mike to Red Bank? And once the idea, the fantastic idea, presented itself, the supporting evidence began to fit like pieces of a puzzle.

The case against Summers and Tommy could apply as well to Allan. All three had been victims of Hatfield's "private charities" with their attendant humiliations and their built-in failures. Allan, like Summers and Tommy, had known Luisa. Like the others he could have fallen a victim to her. He had been bitter about the display room and the fact that he had

218

no money. He must have wanted it for the greedy hands of that vicious woman. Then, all at once, he had talked confidently of money rolling in soon. Hatfield money instead of legitimate profits from his ceramics? I recalled the difference in him when he came back at the time of my parents' death, how haggard he had become. If he had fallen into Luisa's hands, that would account for a lot. And in all those months while he had divided his time between the Red Bank shop and his display room on Manhattan, he had not attempted to get in touch with us.

Clark said abruptly, "I'm going to make some calls. I'll be back. You wait right here." Apparently he did not hear me suggest that he use my phone. I saw his long legs scissoring past the window. It was some time before he returned.

"I've been wondering," I told him, "why Allan asked me to marry him after my parents died if he was in love with Luisa. Why?"

Clark was amused. "I can think of a lot of reasons."

"But I could never compete with Luisa."

His amusement deepened. "You underrate yourself shockingly, Kate. Luisa knew better. That's why she was so determined to get you out of circulation."

"But it was Tommy she wanted. I told her that I was going to marry Allan; that I wasn't interested in Tommy."

"But that wasn't the truth, was it?" Clark said gently. "Well, it's not too hard to understand Allan's point of view. I imagine in the beginning he realized he was getting too deep into something he couldn't handle. He was probably obsessed by the woman, but that isn't love, you know. You were to be his escape, his attempt to shake free of her before it was too late. He's the kind of guy, or at least that's the way I

219

summed him up, who basically wants to stay in line. It would take tremendous pressure to make him break his pattern. I could find it in my heart to be sorry for the guy. He must have lived in hell, and all for nothing."

"If he's the one who abducted my brother, I can't be sorry for him. Even if we find Mike—in time, I mean—he'll never be the same again, never trust anyone after he admired Allan so much."

"Oh, don't be silly, Kate. Kids are a lot more resilient than you seem to think. Hell, the whole human race is or it would never have survived the unspeakable ordeals of acute hunger, great pain, and all the catastrophes flesh is heir to."

"Well, maybe." I wasn't convinced. "But a man who could batter another man to death—"

"I'm not condoning anything," Clark said. "All I'm trying to tell you is that Allan's been paying for it with every breath he drew. First, Luisa persuaded him to kill Hatfield, promising him herself and the money. He killed Hatfield, and all his hatred and envy and disappointment came through in that beating. And then he discovered that little Mike had witnessed the crime and he had to take him away; something unexpected, something shattering because he didn't want to hurt the boy. He simply wanted to save his own neck. Then he found out that Luisa had no intention of marrying him, that it was Tommy she wanted."

Clark looked at me and shook his head, half smiling. "I'm not condoning the guy, Kate. I'm trying to explain what I believe happened. Well, the next thing is that Summers found out, as Allan had done, that Luisa was after Tommy and he believed that it was Tommy and Luisa, not Allan and Luisa, who had planned the murder. So he brought pressure to bear and forced Luisa to give him that promissory note and tried to get a cut out of Tommy too. But Luisa wasn't bluffed. She went to Summers's hotel and shot him in the back of the head while he slept. And then she couldn't find that note.

"So yesterday, in desperation, she put the screws on Allan to get back that note for her, promising to give him the same amount—if he eliminated Mike and you."

"And so Allan was the one who pushed me down the stairs."

Clark shook his head. "You were alone when you started down those stairs, Kate, and nervous as a cat, starting at every sound. The guy I had keeping an eye on you said there was a car backfire and you leaped, tripped and fell headlong. He was going to look at you when Eakins appeared at your door, wild-eyed, carried you in, and put you on the couch. My man watched until he saw that you were okay."

"I'm glad," I said on a long breath. "Oh, I'm glad." And after a moment, "Do you think Allan poisoned Luisa?"

"Do you mind so terribly?"

"You mean on my own account? Well—"

"You see," Clark said apologetically, "when I suggested that you'd be better off with Allan than with Tommy, I didn't know as much as I do now, not by a long shot. By the time you announced your engagement, I had learned from the Missing Persons Bureau that Allan had done his best to keep the police from looking for Mike. He'd gone to see them before he went in with you, saying that Mike was a habitual runaway. It was his form of holding his breath, a kind of power struggle to get what he wanted. 'Let me do as I please or I'll run away.' According to Allan, it worked every time,

221

but he couldn't say so to you because you wouldn't hear a word against him. You thought he was perfect."

"Mike would laugh at that."

"Well, that got me interested in friend Allan, so when you showed me that ring I was a bit rattled. Especially," and Clark paused for a moment, "when I realized how—joyless —that engagement really was."

"And the other day it was Allan you were having followed, wasn't it?"

"It was Allan."

"Have you found Mike?"

"We'll find him before the day is out. I've suspected for a couple of days that he is at the Red Bank house, but I didn't dare make a move that might—precipitate matters."

"Do you think he's still alive?"

"I don't think Allan wants to kill him. It's my guess that his wish to marry you at once is because he knows Mike would not betray your husband. And I think he is really fond of the kid, just as he is more than fond of you. I believe he loves you." Clark smiled. "You are easy to love, you know. In fact, if it weren't for Tommy, I'd be trying to get you for myself." At my astonished expression his smile deepened and he gave me a brotherly hug. "Never mind. I'm not trying to compete. Anyhow, if I did, Tommy would probably tear me apart."

"Tommy doesn't even like me. He said I'm too young for him and he likes playing around and—"

"He was so—afraid for you, Kate."

"Clark," I went back to the point that was tormenting me, "how on earth did Tommy get hold of Luisa's handkerchief if he was not the one who killed her?"

"I've been wondering about that. When Tommy and I talked this morning—oh, yes, that's where I went to telephone and make some arrangements—"

"You've been holding out on me!"

Clark grinned. "You bet I have! Anything you know you come out with to the next comer. I'm taking no chances until this deal is sewed up. Anyhow, to get back to the handkerchief. Tommy was flabbergasted when I told him it was Luisa's. He said he'd taken it out of your coat pocket to wipe the blood off your head."

"Out of my—but that is ridiculous. I never—oh! While you were calling your office at Allan's, I saw a handkerchief on the chair I was sitting on and I just took for granted it was mine and put it in my pocket."

"Piling up, isn't it?" Clark said cheerfully. "But there's only one piece of concrete evidence so far, until we get hold of Mike. As things stand now, it's mostly guesswork."

"So?"

"Do you remember saying you'd be willing to let me gamble with your safety in order to assure Mike's?"

"Yes."

"This is it, kid. Are you willing to stick your chin out?"

"Yes."

"Then remember this. Whatever happens, you'll be all right. Is that clear? You'll be all right."

"What do you want me to do?"

"Confront Allan."

"Oh!" After a long pause I asked, "How do I do it?"

"That's up to your own mother wits, Kate. How you go about it is for you to decide. I have a little device here you can stick inside your bra, and when you are prepared to

223

record Allan's words, you turn this switch. See?"

"Yes, but he'd notice, especially if he is nervous and frightened."

"We'll get you a flower to pin on your dress and when you fidget with it or rearrange it, or something, you can switch this on or off."

"Get me a red tulip," I said, and he nodded.

"Now how about your plans?"

"Well, Lieutenant Carfare wanted me to go to a hotel tonight. Why don't I take my bag and go out to Allan's for protection? That would be the natural thing to do, wouldn't it? After all, we intended to get our wedding license this week and be married." My voice shook a little.

"Not a bad idea. Now listen to me, Kate. Are you paying attention? All right, then. Mike's safety depends on what you do and say in the next few hours. We've got to have evidence to present to a jury. Don't give yourself away. Think before you speak."

He picked up my bag and carried it out to the rickety old Volkswagen. At a florist's around the corner he got me a red tulip. "The manager didn't think much of me as a customer. Just one tulip. I told her it was all I could afford." He fastened it at the neck of my dress over the little recording device and again made me practice switching it on and off. "And if you turn it off when it's supposed to be on, I'm going to wring your neck," he assured me.

Sunday traffic was light. We drove through the tunnel to the Jersey side where there were only a few cars in evidence, as it was still too early in the season for vacationers.

After a long time I said, "Clark, I'm trying to get my thoughts straightened out. I still can't believe in Allan's

224

complicity in all this. I keep trying to, but it doesn't work. He's not that kind of man. He described himself once as the sort who would be listed on an old-fashioned program as A Friend of the Family. And that's what he is really like."

"What he was like. What he might have remained if it hadn't been for Luisa."

"And that threatening call I got?"

"That was to force you to call off the police search."

"And the call Allan said Mike made from Rochester?"

"That was to get rid of me."

"Was he the one who wrote those threatening letters to Mr. Hatfield?"

"Sure. Another miscalculation. He probably expected Hatfield to turn them over to the police, indicating the existence of an unknown enemy. Instead, Hatfield hit on the idea that it was Tommy, with Summers's able assistance, and he went to the agency to handle the matter by himself."

"Clark!" I exclaimed.

"Hey, don't make me jump like that. I nearly lost control of the wheel."

"I was remembering. After Mike disappeared and I was talking to Allan, he spoke of a green dress I was wearing. He said it was the same color as Mike's sweater. I had knitted them myself and Mike was wearing his for the first time that morning he disappeared. He was dressed up to go to Joe's party."

At a delicatessen, which was doing a fair business for Sunday morning with half a dozen men standing around, Clark went in and spoke briefly, apparently getting the address of the ceramics workshop. He left the car there and we walked on to Allan's shop, a one-story building one room wide and two rooms deep. The building was on a corner with a vacant lot next to it and a dilapidated, deserted building across the street. Anyone could be hidden there for a long time, unobserved and unheard.

Clark looked closely at the unshaded windows. We walked along the driveway and saw a pickup truck parked at the back of the building. The windows in the back room, where Allan had slept before he moved to our house, were heavily curtained. I was so occupied looking at the curtained windows, wondering whether Mike was behind them, that I would have stumbled if it had not been for Clark's grasp of my arm. The object over which I had nearly fallen was a large garbage can and, burned in one side, were the initials P.C., Pietro Caspari, the owner of the restaurant at the end of our alley. Another piece of the puzzle fell into place. At last there was tangible evidence that Allan had been in the alley on that horrible Saturday morning.

"You knew about it?" I whispered.

Clark nodded. "Got the word yesterday. We've just been waiting for a safe way to get in without causing the boy any harm." He handed me the weekend bag. "Okay?"

I nodded, touched the tulip and groped for the gadget inside my bra. Clark put thumb and finger together and I waited until he had gone down the street and around the corner toward the delicatessen. I had never felt so alone in all my life. I opened the door and went in.

II

The shop was typically neat with his equipment behind a large folding screen, and a table holding a few samples. Allan

226

was at a standing desk at the back, absorbed in sketching and looking tired—so tired. As the door opened, he wheeled around and stared at me, jaw dropping.

"Kate!" It took him a moment to collect his wits. He came to meet me, took the weekend bag away and set it down. "What on earth—why didn't you call me?"

I found that I could not meet his eyes, not without shame —shame and pity for him and yet a kind of hate too.

I told him that the police thought I was not safe in the apartment. I'd had a bad fall on the steps, whether pushed or not, and I was knocked out. Tommy was there at the time—

"In your apartment?" Allan demanded.

"Yes. He had a key, of course. And he bathed my forehead with Luisa's handkerchief."

"So that's it," Allan said, and I could see the tight lines of his face relax. I had handed him a perfect stooge. He leaned over and kissed me lightly on the bruised forehead. "Poor darling!"

My flesh crawled at his touch and it required all my will power not to jerk away from him. "The police want me to go to a safe place until they've made an arrest. So naturally I thought of you." I fumbled with the red tulip and switched on the recording gadget.

"But, my dear," Allan said in perplexity, "I can't very well put you up in my apartment. Not until we are married. You know how people are. You'd be much better off at a hotel."

"But can't I stay here? You did until you came to our house to live. And I don't mind if it's not very comfortable. It would be just for one night."

"But, darling, you can't stay here alone. Anyone could

227

break the flimsy locks on the doors. I've never tried to make the place burglar-proof because there's so little to steal. And the place is horribly isolated."

"If there's nothing to attract a burglar, then what is there to be afraid of?"

I could almost hear his thoughts whir. He didn't dare let me stay. And he didn't know how to get rid of me.

"I'll tell you what! We'll go back to New York and I'll find you an inexpensive hotel for a night or two, just until Tommy is safely under the hatches."

"I don't want to go back to New York. I'm sure I could manage here, that I'd be comfortable enough. Let me see for myself, Allan."

His face changed then. "What do you really want, Kate?"

"I want Mike."

Eighteen

From somewhere near at hand there came a frantic drumming of heels.

"Mike!" I shouted. "Mike!"

The drumming became frenzied.

As I started toward the back room, Allan caught my arm, stopping me. He was ghastly. He looked almost as though he were going to faint, but in his eyes there was something I had never seen before. I wished with all my heart that Clark had not left me to face this alone.

"Oh, Kate," Allan groaned, "why did you have to interfere? I haven't hurt him. I would have let him go."

"Would you?"

"But don't you see that when we are married, Mike will never do anything to hurt you—or me, for that matter."

"We'll never be married, Allan." I pulled off his ring and set it down on the drawing board where I saw the sketch he was making of Fillmore Hatfield. Apparently he hoped to make a profit by selling portraits of the dead man to the kind of people who like macabre keepsakes.

"Certainly we're going to be married!" Allan's hand tightened on my arm. "Can't you see that it's the only right and possible thing to do? You were ready to marry me yesterday. Nothing has been changed."

"Nothing?" I said incredulously. "Mr. Hatfield was battered to death, Dan Summers was shot through the head while he slept, Luisa Hatfield died in a taxicab of poison." I saw Allan's startled expression. "You hadn't heard that? In spite of her disguise, she was identified by her fingerprints. She had a record for giving lewd performances. The driver had picked her up on Fifty-seventh Street. She was alone, but the cashier remembered there had been a man with her, a man wearing dark glasses. And all this time you watched me living in hell because Mike had been abducted, you pretended to sympathize, to help me. And you say that nothing has been changed."

"There's only one possible solution now, Kate," Allan said impatiently, and I turned back to face him so that the gadget would pick up his words. I felt more like an avenging angel than like Judas, though I was probably a mixture of both. "Marry me, and we can go on, forgetting all this horror, putting it behind us. My stuff is beginning to take. Luisa"— he caught his breath and then went on—"persuaded Fillmore to plant a glowing article about it and people are beginning to buy. Before long I'll be making enough for more comforts if not for luxuries, even if—"

"Even if you aren't going to collect any of the Hatfield money? You seem to think that once Mike is muzzled by me, you'll be safe, that there will be nothing to fear."

"Why are you coming out with all this, Kate? Don't let your infatuation for Tommy Eakins blind you to the truth.

When the police have built their case against him—"

"With your help," I suggested.

"Why did you come here today?" Allan demanded. "Don't say you were looking for a safe place to sleep."

"I told you. I came for Mike."

His voice changed. "Who knows you are here?"

"I know what you are thinking, Allan. You killed Hatfield out of love for his wife and envy of his money and sheer hatred of the man—and it was all for nothing. You killed Luisa because she had murdered Summers and you realized that she was dangerous. And she wanted you to kill both Mike and me. I heard her talk, Allan, when she called you from her agent's office."

"She used no names," he said quickly and as quickly stopped.

"You wanted to save us. I think you really did. And anyhow you knew Luisa had simply made use of you. And now you think you can make a bargain with me. You'll offer to save Mike—and me—if we'll save you."

There was a long pause while Allan simply looked at me without speaking, the color drained from his face.

"No, Allan, I'm not bargaining. When I think of that darkling hill I've been climbing for the past week, I can't forgive you. Not ever. What have you done to Mike, Allan? If he saw the murder, and of course he must have seen it, you never said, 'Now just come along with me like a good boy, Mike.' He wouldn't have done it. He'd have yelled bloody murder before he'd have let you get away with it. Actually it is Mike who is responsible for catching you. He dropped the dog whistle and someone found it here in Red Bank and mailed it to Joe. Lucky for you, the man carried it around

231

in his pocket until Monday morning when he found it and mailed it in New York. But as soon as he noticed the ad, he telephoned to say where he had found it. You underestimated Mike, Allan, just as you underestimated me."

"Now what do you think happened?" Allan asked, trying to sound as though I were spinning an incredible but amusing tale.

"I think you got the shock of your life when you saw Mike at the window, the first Saturday he had ever been home. I think you knocked him out and put him in a garbage can, which you piled on the pickup truck you'd had waiting until Hatfield came out of the agency. I've just seen the garbage can out in back. It was stolen from the restaurant owner down the alley and has his initials burned into it. It was stolen last Saturday. You'd have a hard time explaining that away. Or explaining how you knew Mike had a green sweater when that was the first time he had ever worn it.

"Allan, the evidence is piling up. In your apartment I found a handkerchief that belonged to Luisa. You lied to the Missing Persons Bureau about Mike, telling them he was an habitual runaway so they wouldn't bother with him. Then when Clark entered the picture, you told me Mike had gone to Rochester as a lark. You really tried hard, Allan, but it's no good."

"Of all the preposterous farrago of nonsense! I can't, for the life of me, imagine how you—or anyone—could regard this seriously as evidence of any crime."

"There's Mike." I pulled away from his restraining hand. "I'm going to get him now, Allan. You can't stop me."

"Oh, Kate. God, I'm so sorry. But I can't let you do it.

You must believe that. I can't let you do it. And yet I love you."

"Yes," I said sadly, "I believe you do. But to save yourself, and to keep Mike from telling what he saw, you are going to kill both of us. Aren't you?"

His face was enough. Allan's kindly face, not basically changed but now stamped with my death warrant.

Where are you, Clark? I called to myself. Tommy! Please, please, Tommy! Even if I'm not your kind, come help me. Now. I'm afraid, Tommy!

"How are you going to do it?" I asked. "Are you going to beat my head in as you did Hatfield's? Are you going to poison Mike and me as you did Luisa?"

"Stop it, Kate! I can't bear this."

"But I'd rather know. Are you going to strangle me or shoot me or knife me—"

"Oh, God," he cried in a kind of agony, "it won't hurt you, Kate. I promise you that."

"You're damned right it won't!" The door was nearly thrown off its hinges and Tommy leaped at Allan, his sheer momentum hurling them both to the floor. I heard Clark shouting as he ran to the two struggling men and a policeman saying in a tone of authority, "All right. Break it up. Let the guy go. We can handle it. Let him go." He laughed. "Leave something for the law."

I didn't wait to hear any more. I opened the door to the back room and for a moment I blinked because it was dark. The heavy curtains drawn across the windows shut out all the light. I fumbled for a switch and a droplight came on, punctuating the darkness rather than supplying useful light.

It was a small room combining the functions of living room, bedroom and kitchen. There was a sagging couch, a shelf holding an electric plate and a few dishes. There was a curtained alcove for clothes.

"Mike!" I called in a panic. Again I heard a drumming of heels. I jerked aside the curtain and there, at last, was Mike. His ankles were tied together, his hands were bound behind his back and fastened by a rope to a heavy hook. He was gagged. His eyes were wide as he stared at me.

Before I could get the gag off, Tommy had joined me, and he was slashing at the cords. He caught the boy as he toppled forward.

Mike croaked as he tried to speak.

"Take it easy, kid," Tommy said as he let Mike down on the couch where he refused to lie, preferring to sit upright. "Get some water, Kate. The boy is parched." Tommy rubbed ankles and wrists vigorously in spite of Mike's moans of pain and protest as the blood started to circulate. It must have hurt a lot.

I brought water, bent over to kiss Mike's rumpled thatch of red hair and, helpfully, burst into tears.

When Mike had finished the glass of water, he was able to talk. By that time a policeman and Clark had crowded into the little room, making it seem smaller than ever. Mike burrowed his head against my shoulder for momentary comfort and then drew away, ashamed of his display of unmanly weakness, but he held tight to my hand.

"Allan?"

"He won't hurt you any more, son," the policeman said grimly.

"Where is he?" The freckles stood out on Mike's face and

at that moment I could have killed Allan myself.

"In the front room, but don't worry. There are two cops with him."

"I guess you'd like something to eat, Mike," Clark said. "Let's get out of here. All right with you, officer?"

"Sure. We're extraditing Drummond to New York to face a murder-one charge." The big officer looked at Mike. "You the one who saw it?"

Mike looked at him, nodded, lost what little color there had been in his face, and then was ignominiously sick. When he had recovered, with Clark's big hand holding his head, and Clark wiping his face with a cool cloth and letting him rinse out his mouth with fresh water, the officer said, "Better get the kid home, miss. We'll have a New York man get his story sometime today. Okay?"

We made a little procession into the main room, the workshop, where we stopped short. A couple of Allan's ceramics had been smashed during the rough-and-tumble with Tommy. Allan stood between two policemen, a welt on his chin, his shirt torn, his hands handcuffed behind him. He did not look frightened. He looked lost and bewildered and utterly spent. As we came into the room, he said, "Mike!"

Mike groped for my hand, refused to look at him.

"Mike," Allan said again, "I want you to know this. I promised Kate to save you if I could. I meant that. I killed Luisa to protect you. It was the only way I could do it. It was for you, Mike. It was for you and Kate."

The policeman who had spoken to Mike was now going through Allan's desk. He pulled out a wallet and a number of papers and keys. "Hatfield's," he said in satisfaction. "I guess that makes a nice neat case."

235

"But there was money in it when I saw him," I said. "A lot of money. It was almost bulging."

"Oh, well, all money looks alike, you know. We never expected to find the money."

Mike spoke then, his voice still hoarse and much too shrill. "Did you kill that man to save me, too, Allan? Did you smash up his face— Oh, I'm going to be sick again," and he lurched into the back room, with Clark beside him.

Allan's eyes followed him, grief-stricken by this new rejection. Even now, with everything smashed, he still saw himself as A Friend of the Family.

II

After a perfectly enormous meal supervised by Tommy, for Clark had gone with the police and Allan, Mike faced a couple of policemen, and no one would have believed he had been a prisoner for eight days, uncertain of his fate, and horrified by the brutal murder done by a man he had trusted. Mike was in his element. He was the center of the stage and he loved every minute of it, which was a relief, because it meant that the hideous experience was not going to have any bad effects. I'd have to watch him like a hawk to keep him from making capital of it.

As we had guessed, he had been looking out of the window when he saw Allan's pickup truck parked near the alley. Then Allan had gone into the alley, called someone, struck the other man with a hammer on the back of the head, turned him over with his foot, and proceeded to smash the face to a pulp. This time, as he told the story, Mike was not sick.

236

Then Allan had turned his head and seen Mike at the window.

"Well, I didn't know what to do," Mike said. "I called Joe to say something had happened and I didn't know how to handle it."

"Why not call the police?" one of the men said. "That's what we're here for, you know."

Mike's flow of words was checked. Then he said, with a shade of uncertainty, "Well, I thought Kate was in love with him. She said once she couldn't tell me how much she owed him. And I didn't want to hurt Kate. She—well, gosh, we're family."

"I see." And I think the policeman did see.

"So then Allan came to the door and before I could say anything, he sliced down hard on my neck. Next I knew I was rattling round in a garbage can and it wasn't clean. Ugh! It smelled beastly."

So did Mike, but no one had the heart to say so. Except Tommy, who said cheerfully, "So do you, kid. A ride in a garbage can does no one any good. As soon as the police are through, you're going into a hot tub and have a shampoo, supervised by me, and I suggest that Kate burn your clothes."

"I don't see what business it is of yours," Mike said, suddenly toppling from a heroic posture to one of a child. "Who are you, anyhow?"

"Well, I—"

"Let's get on with the boy's story," intervened one of the policemen.

"Well, it seemed like there was nothing I could do, but I

wouldn't buy that. I didn't have more than five cents in my pockets, a couple of soiled handkerchiefs, a penknife and that dog whistle I'd bought for Joe. It was addressed, you know, so I figured if I had a chance I'd toss it out and someone might stamp and mail it so you'd know I was in Red Bank. So when he was trying to get me out of the can, he was so busy gagging me he didn't notice when I dropped the whistle."

"Nice thinking," the policeman said and Mike preened himself. I could see trouble looming ahead when I'd have to cut him down to size. But I was so proud of his stamina and his lack of self-pity, and I so loved his dirty little face and his whole smelly person, that I could do nothing but beam fatuously at him.

"Of course," and the self-satisfaction faded, "after a while I figured no one found the whistle or someone just pocketed it."

On the whole, he said, it hadn't been too bad. Allan let him go to the bathroom and brought him food twice a day, real sharp food like frankfurters and French fried potatoes and Coke, only he got kind of tired of having them twice a day. Allan kept him tied to the bed most of the time, but when people might be dropping in he tied and gagged him in the closet. That was the worst part. The dark. The discomfort. The waiting. The—Mike would rather have died than use the word fear.

"Of course I knew Kate was bound to find me. Or Joe."

And at last the police left, taking Mike's statement with them, and shaking his filthy paw solemnly. He was to go to the precinct in the morning to sign the statement. There was one uneasy moment when I could see the whites of his eyes

238

like a startled horse.

"Will Allan be there?"

"He will not be there," the policeman assured him. "He'll be plenty busy somewhere else." He turned to me and held out his hand. "Now if I can have that gadget of yours, miss." I unfastened it and gave it to him. "Nice piece of work you did there, you and the kid. You're tops, the both of you."

"Officer," Mike said, emboldened by this praise, "can I bring my friend Joe with me to the station?"

At his ecstatic expression the policeman struggled to keep a straight face. "Delighted," he said, and Mike's cup ran over.

"If I had known," Tommy said furiously after the officers had gone, "how Clark was using you, I'd have taken him apart."

By then my spirits were rocketing. I laughed at him. "I'd like to see you try."

When Mike had been scrubbed from head to foot by a ruthless and unrelenting Tommy, after putting up a strenuous fuss at submitting to discipline after having led a life of adventure and being congratulated by the police, Tommy sat on. By then I knew that Clark had taken him into his confidence and they had both gone to the police Saturday night when Tommy had told them everything he knew.

"Though why I couldn't have been let in on it," I said in disgust, "I don't know."

"Because, my sweet Kate, you'd have babbled every word of it to Allan before we could close in."

"Well," I said at last, "I'm going to bed and get a good night's rest and tomorrow I'm going job hunting."

"Why?"

"You fired me yesterday. Remember?"

"Oh, that," he said airily.

"Yes, that!"

Tommy settled himself on the couch beside me and put his arm around me.

"I'm not your type, remember?"

He grinned. "I must have been thinking about someone else." The laughter was back in his eyes and he held his head at its old jaunty angle. There was purpose in his face as he began to tighten his arm around me, to tilt up my chin with a gentle hand. Tommy and his damned, irresistible charm, knowing just how effective it was.

"I must say," I said hastily, to say something, anything, because my heart was thumping and I had no intention of letting Tommy think he could throw me down and pick me up at will, "Mike is insufferably conceited about the whole thing. He can't wait for morning when he is going to play star part with the police and show off for Joe. I'm going to have a time with him."

"What you need," Tommy told me, "is a man around the house to enforce discipline." To demonstrate what he meant, he kissed me—long, drowsy kisses, to which, to my fury, I found myself responding with enthusiasm.

When I could breathe again, I said as calmly as I could, for I was a bit breathless, "Discipline? You?"

"Maybe," and there was humility warring with the challenge now, seriousness tempering the laughter, "I can do better with him than I did with myself. Do you think so, Kate?" He held me off to look at me and there was anxiety and an appeal in his face.

240

And demonstrating my treachery to all womankind, I said basely, "I don't want you any different, Tommy. Just as you are!"

Well, after all, I asked for it.